Future Bristol
Edited by
Colin Harvey

Swimming Kangaroo Books
Arlington, Texas

Dive into a good book at
www.swimmingkangaroo.com

Future Bristol
Swimming Kangaroo Books, April 2009

Swimming Kangaroo Books
Arlington, Texas
ISBN: Paperback 978-1-934041-93-2

Other available formats: PDF, HTML, Mobi (No ISBN's are
assigned)

LCCN: 2009920026
British Library Cataloguing in Publication Data.
A catalogue record for this book is available from the
British Library.

Cover art by Andy Bigwood

For Georgia, Julius, and all the good people of the
Exeter University SF Society, who unwittingly played
their part in the creation of this book.

Books by Colin Harvey

Lightning Days

The Silk Palace

Vengeance

Blind Faith

Anthologies Edited by Colin Harvey

Killers

Coming in Fall 2009

Displacement

Contents

		Page
Introduction		iv
Isambard's Kingdom	Liz Williams	1
The Guerilla Infrastructure HOWTO	John Hawkes-Reed	21
After the Change	Stephanie Burgis	48
A Tale of Two Cities	Christina Lake	70
Trespassers	Nick Walters	97
Pirates of the Cumberland Basin	Joanne Hall	125
Thermoclines	Colin Harvey	153
What Would Nicolas Cage Have Done?	Gareth L Powell	181
The Sun in the Bone House	Jim Mortimore	201
About the Contributors		229

This page is provided for messages from those
who wish to give the book as a present to a friend.

Introduction

This book was born of strange parents; civic pride isn't so unusual, especially for "Blow-ins" as native Bristolians describe anyone who wasn't born around the confluence of England, Wales, and a narrow portion of the Atlantic Ocean (you can have lived ninety-eight out of ninety-nine years of your life in the city and still be a Blow-in), who tend to wax more lyrical about their adopted city than natives.

There's a lot to wax lyrical about; this is the city that gave the world Concorde, the doomed but beautiful Brabazon airliner, the elegant Bristol 410 saloon; Methodism; Massive Attack and Portishead; the SS *Great Britain*—so ahead of its time it was an SF-nal ship—Clifton Suspension Bridge and other bits of Brunel's relentless innovation, and...Oh I could go on and on, but I won't. Google it, instead.

But when I moved here almost thirty years ago, Bristol—like much of the UK—was going through a crisis of confidence as the old certainties of Cold War and industrialization began to crumble. It became a familiar refrain, that, "We don't actually make anything any more." As if house-bricks and *things* are all that there is to life.

Well, we do actually make things, albeit things that are hard to measure. Here are some of them.

That brings me to the other, stranger parent; isolation.

Writers work alone, as a rule. Even collaborations tend to be written via e-mail, and the writer's life is a solitary one. For ten years I believed myself to be the only SF writer in Bristol, but that was because I wasn't looking in the right places. Then two years ago, more by accident than design, I attended a convention in Exeter, and met three of the contributors to this anthology.

So the two parents met and spawned this anthology. It's a celebration of the city that we moan about but also love. A city that, like British SF, believes in itself again, which is perhaps why it's been picked up by an American publisher, which is appropriate, given that the voyage that saw the discovery of continental America started from Bristol in 1497.

Because the USA, as reflected in its SF, is experiencing a similar crisis of confidence to that felt by Britain in the latter half of the last century, as the old certainties falter before an emerging Asia and a resurgent Russia. British SF shows that crises can be surmounted. It took us a long time to recover from the loss of Empire, but there's a renewed buzz, even a swagger in British SF. We're looking forward, not back.

But this book is also a flare sent up to any other writers working in isolation; *here we are, come and find us. We're over here!*

The contributors in this book come from all sectors, TV tie-ins to epic fantasy, short-stories, and novels. There are award-winners and debutants, all coming together to celebrate the city that is—or was, in some cases—their home or work place.

Here are some of the things we make.

Colin Harvey

Isambard's Kingdom

By Liz Williams

i.

The sphinx smiles down at me, flexes an immense paw. Above, one of the new airships floats overhead, serene as a god. I am standing at the entrance to the bridge, looking out across sparkling mist, waiting. The hem of my robe—the white and crimson of a Welcomer—snaps in the breeze. I lean a little more heavily on my iron staff and smile back at the sphinx. In the reflected metal of the panelling on the tower, our faces are not unalike: broad, dark, patient.

My name is Olaudah Jea. I do not know the sphinx's name, for such things are guarded carefully. I call her *Left Hand*. She sits on the left hand tower, staring into the mist and occasionally, one supposes, conversing with her Right Hand companion.

The mist is glittering, a sign of imminent arrival. I tap the iron shoe of my staff against the iron strut of the bridge, producing an echoing clack. Patient I may be, but sometimes things need to be speeded up a little.

"Mr Kingdom!" I cry. I don't mean to order him around—experts must be respected—but he is like all scientists, prone to wander off into a haze of speculation, diagrams scribbled on the backs of envelopes, on table tops, on bridges. "Mr Kingdom!"

And after a moment, an answer comes.

"Olaudah? Is that you?"

The sphinx's smile widens.

"Who else would it be?" I say.

He steps out of the mist, top hat speckled with droplets of congealed ethereality. "My profound apologies. I was at work on a new device, something quite radical, which the Venturers' Guild will, I am sure, be happy to hear about."

"Another invention, Mr Kingdom?" This is not, absolutely, his name, but it amuses me to call him this and I think it amuses him, too. He points upward, past the sphinxes, past the upright struts of the bridge, to where a thin sickle moon is riding. The airship—her name is *Beginnings*—soars beneath the lunar crescent, her sails outstretched to catch the winds of the Severn Sea. "As graceful as that one?"

"Pah!" Mr Kingdom is too much the gentleman to spit over the side of the bridge, but I can tell that this is his initial reaction. "My creation would take you much further than these upper airs. All the way to *that*, in fact." And his finger stabs directly at the moon.

I do not like to question the mad, or engineers, which amount to the same thing. "Well, that would be a marvel, Mr Kingdom," I say. "Now, about the arrivals..."

There is a little more urgency in my voice now, for I can see their forms starting to emerge through the mist. Their eyes are wide: they must think they are crossing from one hell into another. They are wrong. And I spread my arms wide, to welcome them home.

ii.

There's more to life here than sugar and slavery. People don't believe me when I tell them this: they're a hard people in Bristol, they say, with an eye to the main chance and to money. Merchants and marketers, always looking beyond the rolling hills and the Severn Sea to the lands over the ocean, where there are fortunes to be won and lost.

But I hadn't come to Bristol to make a fortune, not as such. I'd come to build a bridge.

* * *

The river Avon runs through a steep and narrow gorge, a place of crags and cliffs. The town perches at its summit, looking out across bucolic green fields. But though the gorge is narrow, it cannot be easily crossed at any point of its snaking length, and thus the good burghers of Bristol wanted a bridge. Who better to consult for the task than myself, Isambard Kingdom Brunel?

I do not wish to sound arrogant. But if anyone is asked to build a bridge, then surely it must be I, who have spanned the gorge of the Severn in its upper reaches, to such effect that the surrounding village is known as Ironbridge? Who has built the Great Western Railway and laid cables beneath the Atlantic? But I am bragging, of course. All those things came later and besides, matters did not go so well with this particular initial construction. I speak from the perspective of a man much older than the one I am supposed to have become. Have patience with me. I must not get ahead of myself—I am an engineer, after all. Things must be linear, structured, in their place, and so I will begin with the original bridge itself, with that graceful arching span across the Avon, with its sturdy Egyptian pillars.

Originally they asked Telford, the idiots. I suppose it makes a kind of sense; he was then the chief architect of the day, a Name. But Telford went his own sweet way in all things, and the bridge he wanted to build was not the bridge they had in mind. So they asked me, and as a rash young engineer of twenty-four, naturally I agreed, and I blessed the name of William Vick, the rich wine merchant who had decided that what Bristol needed was a bridge.

He had left a thousand pounds to achieve this end, setting it in an account that would enable it to grow. When the sum grew eightfold, the city fathers decided they could wait no longer and summoned first Telford and then myself to the city.

It was my first visit to Bristol, and I knew little of the place. A rural city, if that is not a contradiction in terms, set amongst cow pastures on the muddy banks of the Avon. A city built on slavery, although only a relative handful of black faces had ever set sight on its pale facades compared to the numbers that had been ferried across the Atlantic to the Americas on Bristolian slave ships.

Slavery had itself fallen prey to the abolitionists in the quarter of a century before I was hired to build the bridge. But the smell of it remained along the wharves and dockyards, in the stale waters of the river, in the wealthy mansions that stood above the cramped streets and the filthy inns.

I did not realise, then, how much more of it remained even than that.

* * *

More than a quarter of a century after *that*, and I am dangling from a metal basket, two hundred feet over the sluggish creep of the river. Needless to say, the tide is out. It is a September afternoon, with the early autumn light hanging trapped and golden among the leaves of Leigh Woods. I am accompanied by a boy named Casket, my wife Mary having inexplicably declined to join me in this particular adventure ("Under no circumstances!"). We seek to cross the bridge for the first time.

I say "bridge." In fact, the construction is yet no more than two turrets, influenced by the Luxorian pylons I have seen in engravings, and I think they look very fine. A steel bar, some eight hundred feet long, passes between them, and this is what will become the bridge itself.

Casket looks down and grows a shade paler.

"Mr Brunel? Why aren't we moving? Have you halted this cradle to admire the view?"

A good question. In fact, although the view this afternoon is also very fine, I have not stopped the basket in order to contemplate it.

Rather, we have stuck.

I am reluctant to inform Casket of this basic fact, but he wants to be an engineer, like me, and he needs to have an empirical approach to reality. Thus, I let him know that through no calculation of my own, we cannot progress any further without someone climbing up the chain that attaches the basket to the iron bar and releasing the bolts.

This someone, I also inform him, had better be me, since I do at least possess the advantage of knowing more or less what I am doing.

Casket, perhaps understandably, is alarmed. What, he asks me, should become of him if I fall?

Well, I tell him, then I will be a corpse floating down the Avon and you will still be stuck, in which unfortunate case someone will have to crawl across that bar with a rope.

Try not to fall, Casket says, with more wryness than I might have expected of the lad under such circumstances. Endeavouring not to look down, I stand on the wavering edge of the basket and begin to inch my way up the chain like a monkey of the Indies.

The basket sways alarmingly and the river, when I do eventually glance down, looks much further away than two hundred feet. I am relieved that my dear wife elected not to accompany me, though I am annoyed that she seems, thus far, to have been proved right. When I look back up again I see that a mist is beginning to appear, boiling down from the length of the iron bar.

Even more annoying. If a mist is coming in—as happens in September when one is not far from a major estuary—the chain will become slippery and I am not that confident of my ultimate dexterity. However, we have no choice.

As I progress up the chain, I see something waving at the corner of my eye. I grip the chain tightly and look across. It is a fragment of red flannel, wielded like a flag.

Odd. Perhaps something has caught on the bridge, and is flapping in the wind—but there is remarkably little wind now, and the mist is descending fast. I go hand over hand up the chain and soon, to my relief, reach the bar.

Except the bar isn't there any more. Instead, I crawl out into a wide plain of gleaming metal, the colour of mother of pearl.

I stand, bewildered. I do not understand what has happened. Then, out of the mist, a voice bids me, "Good afternoon!"

I turn. A man is standing on the bridge. He is as black-skinned as any Caribbean slave and he wears a flowing robe of red and white, plus a small round skullcap. He carries an iron staff. He is beaming.

"Mr Brunel?"

"Yes. How do you know my name?"

"Ah. Well, we have met before, you see. Or rather, after. In fact, we know one another quite well."

"My dear sir," I say, "I fear that I have never seen you before in my life and I feel certain that I would have remembered you."

The man gives a slight bow. "This is mysterious, I know. However, I hope to make it a little more plain. Please come with me."

After a moment's hesitation, I do so. I follow the swirling red and white robes to a point at the end of the bridge—for such it must surely be. As we walk, the mist whirls upwards and a tower emerges from it—a tower that is very familiar to me, having been built from my own drawings and with its twin on the Leigh Woods side of the bank, now forming the only completed part of the bridge.

My tower, and yet not quite my tower. Whereas my own edifice had been constructed from brick, this is clad in a softly gleaming metal, darker than that beneath my feet, a kind of shimmering bronze shot with green lights, like a beetle's wing. And on top of it—I gasp.

I've always liked sphinxes. I had hoped, all those years ago, that the city fathers would have let me have a couple on the towers of the bridge, for they are very fashionable, and they had appeared in my original specifications. But— bah!—it had been deemed too expensive and thus my towers sat, sphinx-less.

Here, however, is a sphinx and although it is the colour of bronze, with a more golden hue than the tower itself, it is alive. Huge sun-coloured eyes blink down at me and then the thing gives a snapping yawn like a cat.

"Please do not think you are boring her," my guide says with a laugh. "She has been awake for some time."

"What is she?" And then, because this seems rude, I say to the sphinx, "Who are you?"

"I am a Holder-of-Place," the sphinx says in a booming, accented voice. For a moment, I think this might be a riddle, like the story of Oedipus, but it seems that this is a simple description of her role, for the sphinx says no more.

"Where is this place?" The images before me are interfering with my engineerial sensibilities: I simply cannot make sense of what I am seeing, and that offends me. It occurs to me that perhaps I have dropped off to sleep in the basket and am dreaming, but if so, I am unable to rouse myself from it. It also strikes me that maybe I have fallen to my death, and unremembering the actual event, have passed into some curious afterlife. I say as much to my guide and he laughs.

"Not at all. You are as alive as I."

This does not help a great deal. He goes on, "But I must introduce myself. My name is Olaudah Jea, and I am a member of the Venturers' Guild."

"You must pardon me," I say carefully, "but I do not think that the Venturers' Guild would allow one of your...colour within their ranks. Make no mistake, I do not approve of these claims as to the inferiority of your kind. I am in favour of abolition. I believe all men may be equal, no matter what the shade of their skin."

Olaudah Jea gives a small, acknowledging bow. "Then you are an enlightened man for your time, Mr Brunel, and I commend you for it. But you are quite correct. In your day, a dog would have had a better chance of joining the city's elite."

"This is not, then, my day," I say. "Is it?"

"No, it is not."

There is a long silence, while I stare at the glistening metal at my feet. "This *is* my bridge, though?" I sound like a child. I feel as though I am clutching at the thinnest of straws, not at the impressive construction on which I am standing.

"Yes, Mr Brunel." Olaudah's voice rings out firm and convincing, dispelling some of the mist in my mind. "Have no fear. You will build your bridge...or rather," he hesitates, and an odd expression crosses his face. "You may remain reassured that your bridge will be built. You have already gone through much travail in the construction of it."

"You might say that," I remark with some bitterness, for truly, with all the projects with which I have now been involved, the Bristol suspension bridge has been the most aggravating: the most subject to delays, stupidities, and hitches. It cheers me greatly to hear this man tell me that it will be successful. And I believe him. I am standing on it, am I not?

"Now," Olaudah continues. "I want you to build me something."

This takes me aback. "But if this is some future time..." I falter. "Surely you have progressed beyond my meagre talents. In my own day, my bridge is not even complete and it has taken years." I could not resist adding with some bitterness, "I sometimes despair that it will ever be finished, regardless of what we might be standing on now."

Olaudah looks grave. "This is *a* future time. I do not say it is *your* future—the future of your world."

"How is that possible?"

"Futures depend on the choices men make," Olaudah says. "In this day, the time in which we now stand, such things are much more closely studied and better understood. Social decisions and policies, with the weight of a society's will behind them, are sufficient to cause the temporal fabric to change course, like a tributary hiving off from a main river." He looks down as he speaks and when I follow his gaze beyond the bridge I see that the mist has cleared. The Avon flows below, higher and therefore wider than in my own day. A ship, with sails as delicate as spider-webs, glides beneath it, heading for the Severn Sea.

"She is heading for the Windwards," Olaudah says. "She carries a substance which is unknown in your day and she is powered by the sun. This is the world in which we find ourselves. And *this*, Mr Brunel, is what I want you to do..."

* * *

I remember that first meeting with my Mr Kingdom as I sit in the watchtower, beneath the guardian gaze of the sphinx, and put a call across the aether to London about the new arrivals. How strange Mr Kingdom seemed, on that first day, a figure from the past, dishevelled, a little afraid, but ultimately at home in the knowledge of his own competence. What I was asking him to do was not easy, and I suspected even then that he would meet with opposition, although I did not know what kind it would be.

Once I have completed my work for the day, I lock the watchtower and walk back across Stone Down, enjoying the evening air. It is late spring now. Daffodils line the walkways and blackthorn laces the hedgerow like seafoam. I have been to many places on this Earth: to the yellow lands of Dahomey and Punt, to many of our island colonies, with their prospering towns and abundant fields, but the beauty of this country can still arrest me in my tracks. I am, I suppose, quintessentially English, born in the West Country and even now disliking to move far from it.

I cross into Clifton, greeting friends and associates at the pavement cafes, shaking hands here and then, but I do not stop. The tall cream house near the park is waiting for me. The key in my bracelet activates the door as I approach and it swings open to familiarity, the cool, sparsely furnished rooms, the sounds of my children's voices. My wife, elegant in her djellebeah and headscarf, smiles at me from the study: she has been working from home today on a case for the Legal Society. We are respectable, affluent, English, fortunate. In Mr Kingdom's day, this house belonged to a man named John Penney, who made his money from the Caribbean, just as I have done. But not in the same way.

* * *

I am clambering back into the basket, my hands raw from the chain. Casket is white-faced beside me. The basket rattles on, heading smoothly for the Leigh Woods tower, and I blink in a sudden shaft of late sunlight.

Casket reaches out and in an uncharacteristic display of emotion, pumps my hand. "Magnificent, Mr Brunel! Well done!"

"What?"

"You did not hesitate! Up, and a manoeuvre with the bolts, and then we were free! Soon we will be standing on solid ground once again, and I confess that I shall not be sorry."

I look up. The basket is trundling along the metal bar, the small wheels moving swiftly and easily. The memories are clear in my mind: Olaudah standing on the bridge, regal in his red and white robes, raising a hand to bid me farewell. And my task— the enormity of it stuns me. I do not think I am capable, but Olaudah believes in me and indeed, he must: his own existence depends upon it.

I am an engineer and an architect, not a philosopher. I do not understand these considerations of the temporal, these loops and wheels of time which are so different from the cogs and gears of my own science. But Olaudah trusts me, I think as the gilded leaves of the Leigh Woods shore come close enough to touch and willing hands reach out to pull the basket to safety. And I trust Olaudah.

That night, the first attack comes.

* * *

I am not one to suffer greatly from nightmares. The nature of my work ensures that I am tired by the time my head strikes the pillow, and my devoted Mary does her utmost to ensure that I get sufficient sleep. Thus, the dream is unexpected, and quite peculiar in its intensity.

I am standing once more on the bridge. But although the towers are similar, there is no broad band of gleaming metal here, no sphinxes. Instead, the road that stretches before me is made of some stony substance, a dark grey in colour, although it is hard to tell through the twilight and the rain, which hammers onto the bridge like gunfire. Down the middle of the road are painted broken white lines and at the far end, which I recognise to be the Leigh Woods side, are two bright lights, yellow in colour.

Voices are shouting. It is a moment before I realise what they are saying.

"You are under arrest!" It is a male voice, harsh and much louder than it should be, booming into my ears.

"I –"

"Approach the checkpoint with your hands raised! If you do not comply, you will be shot."

I half turn around, but there is no one behind me. They must be talking to me. I do as I am instructed and walk forwards. Soon I am close enough to hear a muttered conversation.

"Your name?"

"Isambard Kingdom Brunel."

A gate—I did not ask for such gates to be placed on my bridge—rattles open with a gaol-house clatter. A figure steps onto the bridge, very different from Olaudah's towering form. This man is equally tall, but wears a garment-like armour that reflects the glaring lights in a wash of wetness. His face is hidden by a helmet. He carries something long and black, but it is not a musket: it is the wrong shape.

"Keep your hands in the air!" he snaps. I do so and my person is briefly and efficiently investigated. My arms are jerked down and bound behind my back with a click of metal.

Then I am taken inside the western tower and read a statement, which speaks of the Nation of Albion and asks me to sign a piece of paper called a Purity Claim. A drop of my blood is taken, so that they may check it for impurities, though I do not know what they mean by this. Then I am bundled inside a cell and told to wait. Snatches of conversation come to me through the bars.

"...some lunatic, impersonating a historical figure..."

"...not so sure, was speaking to one of the state scientists last week..."

"...enemies are known to have crossed the temporal gap..."

"...cannot risk an incursion..."

Later, I hear my first captor's voice, speaking through a device to someone in London. I am to be taken there and—there is a small spark of light. I look up. The ceiling of the cell has become transparent. Far above it, golden eyes blink down at me.

"Mr Kingdom," the sphinx's voice says to me, as warm as sunlight, "they will try to reach you through sleep. Do not let them. You must wake up."

I try, but how do you rouse yourself from a dream?

"I cannot—"

"Wake!" roars the sphinx, and I am there in my bed, clammy and shaking. I do not sleep for the remainder of that night.

Future Bristol

* * *

It happens again and again, although I never once reach the guardhouse on the bridge. Everything else is the same: the wet road, the lights, the shouting voices. And I feel as though I am watched, figures glimpsed at street corners from the edges of my eye, shadows in the night, strange sounds. My health suffers and so does the bridge, which despite an ecstatic mention in the local press, is languishing. The original legacy has long since run its course and we are dependent upon city funds, which are slow to appear.

I go north, south, east. I build other things: bridges, tunnels, steamships. I become famous and not a little wealthy, but the Bristol bridge is never far from my mind, and nor are the things that Olaudah told me. I have a secret work, now, a work which I practice at night when my family sleeps. I myself sleep little, and I never know if someone is looking over my shoulder; Olaudah is not here, to tell me what to do, though I have often stood at the tower on the Stone Down side and called his name. Often, too, I think I have imagined him—such an unlikely dream—but besides, there are the calculations that he gave me.

It is not a science I understand. It seems made up of more than simply mathematics, for there are words within it, too, more suited to poetry than architecture. "To be free" are such words, and "beauty", and others in a language that I do not comprehend. Olaudah told me, when he handed over the specifications, that it did not matter whether I understood all the material; all I had to do was to set the calculations down and work them through.

"If I don't know what I'm doing," I said to him, "then this may take years." And Olaudah sighed and said that yes, this was indeed true, but he offered me no other recourse.

It is hard to describe the calculations themselves. I work at them, and then return next morning to find that the figures seem to have rearranged themselves on the page, forming other configurations which I must then puzzle out. Sometimes, before my tired eyes, images rise from the page and float away: glimpses of islands set in a sapphire sea, a long yellow coastline. Sometimes I hear what sounds like the clank of an iron chain, or glimpse a fragment of red flannel fluttering out of the corners of my eyes.

Years after I first set sight on Olaudah, I return to Bristol. I have reached the point that he told me I would, where it is necessary to implement the calculations themselves. I made careful note at the time of the manner in which this is to be done, and I have not forgotten.

The bridge is much as I had left it. There is more than the iron bar, now, for some structure has been erected, a kind of scaffolding, and it is possible to walk out a little way onto this. Following Olaudah's instructions, I have inscribed the latest working into a small metal tablet. I am to place this upon the structure of the bridge.

I do so. It is a November morning, the winter sun striking harsh notes from the scaffolding and from the trickle of the river below. Into this silvery world I place the tablet. I am hoping to see Olaudah once more, but instead, it is the world of the dream that finds me.

Immediately I am convinced that I have done something wrong. It is dark, but it is morning rather than evening. There is a bloody smear of sun to the east and thunderheads mass over the Severn Sea. A pair of lights rushes towards me, and there is a booming, blaring sound. I throw myself out of its way and crack my arm painfully against the iron sides of the bridge. More machines are coming, pouring across the bridge onto the Leigh Woods side.

"Olaudah!" I cry. "Olaudah, help me!" And something cuffs me to the ground. I sprawl on pale metal, and when I look up, it is into golden eyes.

"Olaudah!" But it's gone and I'm lying on the floor of the Stone Down tower, my cheek pressed against the ground. Passing outside to the scaffolding, I see that it is dusk, a wintry light fading fast over the west. The scaffolding looks no different and I cannot see the tablet: it must have fallen into the river below. With a cold, sinking sensation of despair, I turn and go back to the town.

I have failed Olaudah. Again and over again, I ask myself why this should matter so much to me. A phantasm, glimpsed years before, a different world. Surely nothing that is real...

But then there is another attack.

It comes, strangely, not at night or during my work on the bridge, but three days later, at a party for my eldest son. One moment I am working a puppet for the boy, the strings dancing in my hands, and the next, I am back on the bridge in the rain. The guardhouse is some distance away, but the gates are open. The machines that rumbled through it have now ceased to do so, but I hear a shout and there is a sharp sudden crack. Something is tumbling through the air towards me, flipping over and over, and before I can dodge it, it strikes me in the throat.

Then, back again, with the children clamouring for more of the puppet and my wife walking into the room with a jug of milk. When I stop choking, I tell her I have swallowed a half sovereign during a party trick, the best excuse I can make.

Naturally, she thinks I am an idiot, but this view changes to concern as the night wears on and my breathing becomes more difficult. There is nothing to feel, nothing to cough up, and yet whatever struck me in that other world of the bridge is still here, lodged within my body. We take increasingly desperate measures to remove the object—forceps, a board to which I am strapped and turned upside down. A ludicrous situation for an engineer, obliged to invent devices to keep me alive. The latter equipment, however, works: something tumbles from my throat and is gone into the air. Over the next few months, my health continues to deteriorate.

And still the bridge is not finished. I truly despair, now, of ever seeing it fully built. Olaudah's dreams, my own dreams—nothing more than ash in the wind. I am no longer able to work—my health is too poor—and so, while I am still able, I return to Bristol and the bridge.

If they have attempted to kill me, in that rainy world, they have succeeded, I think as I stand at the Stone Down tower. My hands tremble as I unlock the door and step through. I have left specific instructions for my wife, on how to present my death to the world. If they want me, I think, then let them take me. I shut my eyes and walk out onto the scaffold.

As soon as I feel rain on my face I know that I am there. I open my eyes and there it is: the guardhouse, with the tall soldier waiting.

"You!" I shout. I do not wait for him to notice me.

He turns and the gun comes up. I do not wait for this, either. I throw myself over the side of the bridge and down.

The cold air hits me like a blow. I can see the glint of the river beneath, but it isn't water any longer. It's metal. It knocks the breath out of me.

"Mr Kingdom!" Olaudah says. "You have arrived!"

Smiling, he helps me to my feet. The bridge is as I first saw it, all those years before. The sphinx blinks in the afternoon sunlight.

"I thought I was dead," I say. The river looks very far away.

"Why, so you are. At least, as your day sees it. We have a somewhat different view of things, in mine. Look." He gestures. "Do you see how your device is working?"

At the middle of the bridge, there is a mist. It sparkles with lights. I see a cascade of numbers, of words, of shapes and patterns. All these sink down into a metal plate set into the centre of the bridge.

"My tablet!" I say. "It was not lost."

"No. It passed from one world to another, to here, and it opens the way, for the arrivals to come through."

The first of them steps out of the mist as I watch. Ragged, in chains, wondering, bewildered.

"Who are they?"

"They are the slaves of your day. Those who passed through Bristol, those who were carried on Bristol's ships. Through your device we have tracked them, diverted them. These are living folk, Mr Kingdom, which you are not. And we have changed the world."

"The other world, the one in the rain?"

"A different Britain. One that might have been and now will never be. You have closed it off. Do you remember what I told you, that our science today is made from the decisions of men? Your decision to trust me was the key. A man who might just as well have been a dream, and yet you trusted me. It changed things, and you see the change before you."

I do not know what to say. Instead, I stand on the bridge, with the golden-eyed sphinx smiling above me and the man smiling beside and watch the arrivals come home.

The Guerilla Infrastructure HOWTO

By John Hawkes-Reed

I was making a charge up the Gloucester road when a dozy sod in a BMW hybrid pulled away from the kerb without looking. If I'd been alert, I'd have spotted the twitch of the front wheel as the driver spotted a gap in the traffic and started to pull out. However, the cycle path and bus lane there funnel into a single uphill section with everything else, and the only safe course of action is to get out of the way as fast as possible. Usually.

There was an ugly sideways lurch as his front wing collected my rear wheel, a flash of grey sky and some Horfield rooftops, and then a thud as I hit the road. I lay there while competing thoughts of *Bastard* and *That's going to be expensive* fought for space with *Get up and belt him with your U-lock before it starts to hurt.*

A head with a Bluetooth earpiece and a collar and tie loomed over me.

"Are you alright ma...Oh, shit. Sorry love."
Wanker.

I ignored his hand and put a dent in the bonnet of his car as I levered myself upright. I took inventory as the driver jabbered on. The rear wheel on the bike was comprehensively shagged, but that looked like all the damage. I was going to need a new pair of combats and wouldn't be wearing short skirts until the road-rash on my left hip healed. It was my own stupid fault for not concentrating while stamping hard on the pedals away from the junction, but it could have been a lot worse.

"A hundred and fifty quid for the rear wheel, fifty for the combats," I said. There was more of a wobble in my voice than I intended.

He stopped dead and stared at me.

"What?"

"Like I said. Or I shall collect URLs from these nice people and we can all talk to your insurers." I waved at the pedestrians who were pointing mobiles in our direction and busily uploading proceedings to their weblogs or video-sharing sites.

I could almost see his train of thought as the muscles of his face worked. *This bloody dyke probably had her horrible friends waiting anyway. If I lose my rag it'll go viral before lunch. Fuck it. The dealer can grow a new wing and bonnet from stock and two hundred is less than my excess. I hope the cow chokes on it.*

I expected him to protest about having to go to an ATM, but he pulled a handful of notes from his wallet and thrust them at me as if they smelled.

I took the money. He started talking again, but I wasn't interested in listening. I turned to lift the bike onto my shoulder and limp towards the kerb. The nearest bike shop was only three streets away, but the nearest useful one was a lot further than that.

22

* * *

Baz and Welsh Pete found me in the pub a few hours later. I'd been experimenting with over-the-counter painkillers and Bath Ales, so I was in an entirely satisfactory condition. Pete offered to hunt the driver down and trash his car, which was sweet of him, but obviously going to lead back to me. I made a show of declining regretfully and honour was satisfied all round.

"We were going up Easton to see Brian the Brain. Want to come?" said Baz, out of the blue.

I looked at the pair of them. They seemed oddly together. Something was definitely up.

"Sure, but I'm a bit slow on my feet," I said.

Baz grinned.

"S'alright. We've got the van, innit."

* * *

Brian the Brain's place had been a dairy or something in a previous life. Since Easton's tangle of streets firmly resisted gentrification, there were CCTV cameras and floodlights clustered on the outer corner of the house, which was small and squatted in the corner of a large yard faced by sheds and outbuildings. Baz reversed up to a set of double doors, and he and Pete began unloading the crap that filled the back of the van; bales of newspaper, plastic sacks of compost, and buckets of food waste.

I hobbled round to the shed door.

"Did you two knock off a recycling wagon or something?" I asked.

Baz looked at me, vaguely guilty.

"Nah, we swapped them some weed."

Brian emerged from a different shed, looking pleased with himself.

"Alright then, Jax? Up for a bit of civil disobedience? Smart."

I shrugged.

"Yeah, probably. As long as it doesn't involve walking much."

I turned to show him my shredded combats.

"Car?" He wrinkled his brow in sympathy.

"Uh-huh."

"Bastard."

"Uh-huh," I said. "Anyway, what's your plan?"

Brian bowed and made as if to usher me into the nearest shed.

"If madam would care to step this way..."

Madam stepped carefully. My leg had stiffened up again since climbing out of the van.

The inside of the shed was white ceramic-faced brick, and there were massive sections of slate forming benches around three of the walls. Those benches were covered in lab glassware and random-looking electronics. There was a distinct atmosphere of...What? Antiseptic? Pear drops? Something far too familiar...Oh. Fuck, no. He wouldn't have.

I stared up at him.

"Jesus. You're not brewing crystal meth are you? That's evil shit. I'm going back to the pub and I'm going to pretend that I don't know any of you bastards."

Brian looked horrified and spread his arms.

"God, no. I mean, fuckin' 'ell, Jax...It's, um. They're two sets of wet-phase nanoassemblers. We're going to grow some trams and the rails to put them on."

24

I folded my arms. Inside, I had that lift-shaft feeling that lives between something going horribly wrong and having to explain it to the relevant authorities. Outside, well, no one needed to know about the inside stuff.

"Riiight. What is it really?"

Brian looked earnestly back at me.

"Seriously."

"Seriously?"

"Look, Jax. How long have you lived here?"

I counted back in my head.

"Um. Four years?"

We all used to be something else.

Brian used to be in biological research. He never said what sort, even when shambling drunk, but the gossip had it that he'd been the sort that would have been dosing squaddies with LSD in less (or more, depending on the gossiper) enlightened times. Welsh Pete used to make things in a factory. It sounded so strangely 19th century to me that I was always too embarrassed to ask him about it, in case I came across like some middle-class cow. Baz had been a radar tech in the Royal Engineers. He was another one who didn't talk much about his past, but the stories he did tell sounded like a whole pile of no fun at all.

I'd been one of the backroom girls employed to make sure an energy company's secrets remained secret, until I burned out. Although it had been less of a burn out and a lot more of a burst violently into flames.

One of those secrets had been kept in a lab that some wag had named the Over-Unity building. I'd been some way up the security pissing-order, but all I could do there was peer through the armoured glass at the techies in their hazardous environment suits. They'd been trying to make something horribly similar to Brian's nanoassemblers behave itself without it eating into the fabric of the building in the process. Organic chemistry has a very distinctive smell, and the atmosphere in Brian's shed was reminding me forcibly of the big biohazard logos that had been plastered on every wall in that lab, next to the decontamination procedures that boiled down to "Try not to whimper when dying. It puts everyone else off." Whatever Brian was keeping had to be one of the docile versions.

"So in those four years, has the traffic got worse or better?" he asked.

"Worse than you can imagine," I said.

Brian nodded as if he could see traffic jams in my head. I wasn't thinking about traffic jams so much as being nanoassembled.

"Nothing that the power elites can bring themselves to do has made any difference. It's time for some direct action."

"Trams?" I said, gormlessly.

"Trams. Semi-autonomous and running on fuelcells. Like buses, but with enough train-ness to be trustworthy."

"I...Sorry. Trustworthy?"

Brian smiled.

"Yes. People trust the railways, even when they're rubbish. When you lived in London, did you travel on the Tube or the bus?"

"The Tube, of course," I answered.

He looked a little smug.

"Why?"

I started to say something, then stopped and thought instead.

"Buses just felt, I dunno, like they could lurch off down some random side road and you'd be completely lost. There was no useful map and you didn't know where the stops were. It was just impossible to feel safe...Oh. Right."

"Quite."

He beckoned me over to where there was a black and oddly skeletal object propped against the wall.

"Here's a section of track we grew earlier," he said.

It didn't look much like any railway I'd seen before. The rails seemed more or less right, only laid up from carbon-fibre mat. There weren't sleepers as such, though. They looked like branches; thicker where they grew out of the "rails" and arranged in an irregular, triangulated latticework. There was probably a pattern to it if you stared at a section for long enough. I peered around the back of the thing. There were still lumps of compost encrusting the sections where what looked like roots twined together. It all seemed disturbingly organic, like a great lump of branching fungus, and I didn't feel like getting any closer to it in case the root-parts made a grab for me.

Brian had no such fear and picked the thing up one-handed so he could show it off some more.

"How? I mean, that's...Wow."

I wasn't that lost for words. The phrase "What the hell are you thinking you stupid thieving bastard you'll get us all killed" was never far away.

"How does it work?"

As if I didn't know.

Brian put the section of rail down and waved at the buckets lined up under the middle bench. I peered into one. A brownish sludge peered back.

"Tip one of these buckets of bugs out where you want the rails to start and keep feeding it compost. The microbes suck the carbon out of the compost and surroundings and turn it into railway."

"But..." I started.

"You lay a trail of pheromones where you want the railway to go..."

"But..."

"...And use a different pheromone to turn the bugs off when you've got to where you wanted."

"Bloody hell."

Brian was grinning broadly.

"Good, isn't it?"

I still felt like that section of railway would make a grab for me, so I found a relatively uncluttered section of slate bench out of its reach, leaned carefully, and began enumerating points on my fingers.

"You'll get arrested. Very arrested..."

I was trying to think of a useful objection to causing traffic chaos and pissing off the council and bus operators, but was quickly coming to the conclusion that it was an entirely insane idea that should be carried out as soon as possible. Sooner. The daft bugger had to have found or bred a docile strain; we'd have been previously-walking biomass otherwise.

Brian's grin didn't subside while I stared at that one finger and argued with myself for a while.

"You're all mad, and it hasn't got a hope of working," I said eventually. "Where do I sign up?"

* * *

My phone rang while I was waiting for a bus the next morning. Voice only; not even a cartoon avatar.

"Jacqueline Mauriks?"

Only my mother or people who don't care that they're pissing me off call me that.

"What?"

"Stevens. Compliance Department. You recall the Winchester collaboration cluster?"

I did. It was a pile of Internet-facing computers used by people who had to have one password for everything so they could write it down for their secretaries. Security sign-off for that nightmare had come with a thick pile of caveats and exceptions, and it had been the last thing I'd worked on for the energy company. I wasn't surprised that it was still running; things like that get left alone.

"It seems that experimental data from the Over-Unity building was being stored there in clear breach of procedure. There was an intrusion and we believe that our intellectual property was actively violated."

"Someone's copied your stuff. How's that my problem and why are Compliance interested?" I said.

Security could "strongly recommend" a course of action. Compliance would angle-grind locks, hack through cables, and take equipment away in wheelbarrows. The rumour had been that they badly missed the days when they provided physical security on drilling platforms in remote and unstable areas.

"The sign-off documents on the Winchester system appear incomplete. If there was a criminal investigation before our own internal audit is finished, those documents would have to be handed over to the relevant authorities. Obviously, as long as our intellectual property is carefully monitored, there will be no need for such investigation."

I wanted to throw the phone against the nearest wall. *We still own you. Keep an eye on your mates for us or explain it to the cops.*

"Define carefully monitored," I said deliberately.

"Use your own best judgement. We'll touch base with you on a go-forward basis."

I stared at the phone as if I expected it to admit to making the call up.

There's no such thing as a coincidence. The day after Brian the Brain shows off some stolen biotech, my ex-employers let me know that they can arrange for me to have a very interesting time if I don't keep an eye on those bugs for them.

* * *

A week later, I pedaled slowly down Old Market as dawn broke. The narrow section at the top was still a rough mix of failed businesses and sex shops. I smiled at the saucer-eyed types tottering from one or other of the rainbow-flagged bars further along and wondered how long we'd have in the face of the concerned residents of the recently converted flats at the far wide end. I kept going over the roundabout, swung left past the central medical directorate and then right over the bridge and on towards the Fleece. A contraption bolted to the back of my bike hissed aerosol pig pheromones onto the tarmac wherever I went. Someone with a similar rig on her bike waved as she made her way up Victoria Street towards the centre. I waved back and turned left towards Temple Meads station.

There were scores of us. A couple hailed me while I swapped out an empty canister halfway down Coronation Road. We weren't supposed to know who else was involved, but I looked up and smiled automatically, then bent back down over the framework.

I was using my own best judgement in carefully monitoring the situation.

I was down to my last canister as I turned off the road in Speedwell, where the post-war prefabricated houses had been, and into a nondescript trading estate. The huge arched building looked a lot like a lost hangar for a nuke-bomber. The Judas set into one of the loading bay doors that opened as I coasted across the car park and Welsh Pete peered out at me, making sure I was who he thought I was.

It was filled with trams.

With their curved roofs of shiny black composite, they looked insectile. The warm and closed atmosphere of damp compost made me feel as if I was in a vast hatching chamber at the centre of a colony mound. I walked up to the nearest tram and stroked its carapace gingerly. It was startlingly smooth, almost frictionless.

"Go on," said Pete. "Have a look around the thing."

I pressed the *open* button and the door hummed out and sideways. It looked like the inside of a bus. If that bus had been grown from plans drawn up by someone who hated straight lines. There was a distinctly organic quality that brought to mind the shell of a Nautilus. It was probably going to give some people a righteous case of The Fear.

I loved it.

I wandered up the gangway between the seats, stroking the different curvatures and grinning like a loon.

I turned back to see Welsh Pete watching me. His grin matched my own.

"They get everyone like that," he said.

"It's...sexy?"

God. Was public transport giving me the horn?

Pete nodded.

"Voluptuous, according to Brian. He reckons it was a complete mistake, but he liked it so much that he left it."

"So, um, what happens now?" I asked. I had visions of riot-vans filled with coppers descending on teams of Bristolians as they desperately shoveled mulch onto the growing tracks. It would never work and we'd all get locked up forever.

"We feed the railway-bugs until the tracks are grown, obviously."

Brian appeared, pushing an empty wheelbarrow.

"But you can't dump a line of compost down Church Road. The police will get you," I said.

And Stevens will get me. Followed by the police.

"Huh?" Brian looked mystified. Then his expression cleared.

"Oh. No. It doesn't work like that. It grows like a massive fungus. The mycelium will follow the pheromone trail underground until we tell it to stop. Then it, um, blossoms overnight. The rails are the fruiting body. We just have to keep the root-end fed and watered, and all those are in out-of-the-way places."

The world wobbled a bit, and I had to lean against the nearest tram. This wasn't a lark anymore. It was happening.

"That. I mean...It's going to work, isn't it?" I said.

Brian grinned some more.

"I find your lack of faith disturbing, Jax."

* * *

I was having a breather, mid compost-shovel, when the council lorry hove into view.

We were deep in the scrub next to where Mangotsfield station had been, and as the lorry rattled over the rough ground, I turned to the others in dismay.

"I think we're busted."

It was heartbreaking. The railway bugs had been slurping up all the garden waste we could find, and we were only a day or so away from the long weekend that Brian wanted to use for cover.

Baz looked about.

"You what? Where?"

I pointed at the big green lorry 50 meters away.

He burst into laughter.

"You Muppet. That's a recycling wagon."

I glared at him.

"Yeah? So? Those useless sods spread broken jam-jars across my road that shredded my tyres. When I rang to complain, they blamed me for not sorting the stuff into the right boxes. They're out for revenge."

Baz favored me with a look that would have worked better with spectacles to peer over.

"You need to stop reading the evening paper and talk to people some more. Look again; they're on our side."

I looked.

The crew looked like they'd just got back from Glastonbury. Cut-off combats, dreads, army boots and baggy jumpers under hi-viz waistcoats. I was sure I recognized the girl with the matching purple gloves and DMs from the pub.

I was too relieved to yell at him for calling me a Muppet.

The lorry drew up and they began heaving bales of paper and cardboard into the middle of the compost pit. I kept expecting it to bubble or burp or something, but all that happened was that things sank slowly into the pit while far away mutant carbon tendrils grew under a street.

* * *

Brian cornered me at the quiet end of the beer-garden. It was Friday evening and we were having a quiet couple of ales in celebration of no one being arrested yet for crimes against transportation. I hadn't heard anything from my ex-employers either. It was all good. I'd had a feeling that this conversation was going to happen though, ever since someone had mentioned a "diversion" to keep the authorities occupied on the bank holiday Monday night. It obviously wasn't enough that there was a charity run through the centre and the music festival up at Ashton Court. I didn't usually fancy the idea of sunburn, septic facilities and overpriced lager, but walking across the suspension bridge to the other side of the Avon gorge and lying in the park with a few thousand others was starting to look like a diverting alternative to whatever he had in mind.

I tried not to fume quietly until I actually had something to fume about.

"Jax..."

Brian loomed over me. I hate it when men do that. Though breathing in a careless manner would probably earn him a beer bottle in the scrotum in my current mood.

"...You know your way around the Internet, right?"

Here we bloody go.

"Can u be leet haxxor chik kplzthx?" I growled.

"Because we need to stop the CCTV from working for a few hours and I...What?"

I glared up at him.

"You don't hang around many scriptkid...Oh, never mind."

His mystified expression was deepening by the second.

"It means 'Will I be elite hacker-girly, please?' It's the way the kids write on the Net. Useless little sods. Anyway. Do I gather that you'd like me to break a government system? Because you know what that'll look like to the professional paranoids? You might as well go down the cop-shop and grass us all up right now."

Brian had taken a step back and his scrotum was now out of range. I took a long pull on my beer and as per usual had the germ of a plan by the third mouthful. The less I want to solve a problem, the more likely my brain is to go "Here, this will work..."

I waggled the near-empty bottle at him.

"You're lucky. It'll only cost you beer for the rest of the weekend."

Brian's face creased into a massive grin.

"Nice one, Jax. I knew you'd come up with something."

While I waited for him to begin bringing me fresh beer as tribute, I messaged a couple of contacts about renting a small army of zombie PCs for a few hours.

* * *

I freewheeled into Brian's yard at around midnight on Sunday. Pete's van was already parked up in the corner, so I struggled the big gates shut and made for the shed with the light under the door.

Brian cleared me some space on a bench and handed me a mug of coffee. I fired the laptop up, borrowed some unsecured wireless from a house nearby, and connected to the traffic-news site that rebroadcast the footage from many of the council CCTV cameras. I sat back with my coffee and waited.

Baz, who'd been busily feeding pay-as-you-go SIM cards into a selection of old phones, seemed confused by my outwardly relaxed attitude.

"Aren't you supposed to be typing away or something, like they do on the telly?" he asked.

I smiled.

"The people on the telly are rubbish and get caught because they're connected to their control-rig when the bad things start to happen. Someone who didn't want to go to prison would set up a disposable mobile to send a codeword to a chat-room that was being monitored by their zombies. And then they'd hide that mobile in the girls toilet in a busy bar in the centre. Y'know, if there was anyone around who did that sort of thing, which obviously there isn't."

I sipped at my coffee.

"And. You'd have to be a complete idiot to kick everything off at 1 a.m. sharp. People do look at traffic graphs and draw conclusions. I mean, I'm just thinking out loud here."

Baz laughed.

"Ok. Just tell me when to start messaging people."

"You'd best start now," said Brian.

Baz began working through the pile of phones. He'd send one of the built-in smiley pictures to two or three numbers on his scribbled list before stripping out the SIM and dropping the phone into a charity collection bag.

Across the city, people would be tipping buckets of sludge into depleted compost pits and then wandering quietly away.

Some minutes later, one of the traffic-cam feeds stopped updating. It jerked back into life once or twice in the next five minutes. By then a couple more cameras were malfunctioning. Soon none of them were updating any more often than once every few minutes. It looked like a fault that could be anywhere in the network between the cameras themselves and my laptop, which was more or less the plan.

An hour or so after that, the tension was giving me unhappy thoughts. I went to lean against the brickwork at the quiet end of Brian's yard. Ostensibly for some fresh air, but mostly because I wanted to listen for police sirens. Were there any more than usual? Were there any coming this way to batter down the gate, swarm inside, have some more battering, and then lock us all up? I paced, trying very hard not to think like that and failing comprehensively.

Brian joined me.

"Fancy a walk to the end of the road?" he said.

"I dunno. Why?"

I really wanted to be left alone to worry about stuff properly.

"So we can see the fruits of our labours at first hand."

Oh, what the hell. If we weren't in the yard, it would be easier to scarper when the police came.

The two of us walked down to where the side-street joined a slightly more important road. Brian crouched and studied the road surface.

"I think we got here just in time. Look."

We looked. There were a pair of bulges running down the road. At first you either wouldn't have spotted them, or assumed it was the aftermath of roadworks. We watched in silence as the rails grew out of the surface of the road. I'd been expecting cracking and lumps of tarmac as the rails forced their way to the surface, but it was more like watching a film of something melting being played backwards, or as if the surface of the road was made of stiff molasses and the treacle-tide was going out.

* * *

Stevens woke me. He sounded even more detached than the last time.

"Ms. Mauriks. Your concept of careful monitoring leaves something to be desired. The relevant authorities will be made aware of our problem with the Winchester cluster."

"Knock yourselves out." I snapped my phone closed before my voice gave me away.

I sat at the end of Brian's sofa and hugged my knees to my chest. I enjoy feeling like I've been dropped in it as much as the next person, and this time I wasn't coming up with any bright ideas other than packing a bag and running away.

I'd been asleep when the trams boiled out of the warehouses and industrial estates like frantic woodlice.

Like so many others, I watched the footage uploaded to several video-sharing sites and tagged with the URL of Tramspace. By the time I'd levered myself from Brian's sofa and stretched the kinks out of my back, Tramspace had gone utterly viral. The webloggers who fancied themselves opinion-formers didn't know what to make of it. Some called it a free-market triumph but hated its anti-authoritarian nature; others hailed it as a victory for collective action while calling us car-hating eco-fascists.

I was curled up in the corner of a seat and reading some of the more unhinged opinions when the tram rang its bell and began to slow. I glanced up to see a policeman standing in the middle of the tracks and signalling the tram to halt. The tram rang its bell a few more times while decelerating, just to indicate that it was nowhere near a stop and that this sort of behaviour was really not on. It must have taken some serious balls on the part of the copper not to dive out of the way. As it was, he looked somewhat startled when the tram nudged him gently, like a vast black beetle hinting that it would quite like a sugar-lump or two.

I slid down in the seat a little. There was a biggish bloke in front of me to hide behind, but if Stevens had been super-efficient and the copper had a face-tagger application on his mobile and felt like using it, I would become suddenly popular.

The policeman boarded the tram and glared at us in an extra specially authoritarian manner, just in case we might be harbouring thoughts of weblogging the encounter. I certainly wasn't going to spoil the fun by telling him that it was all going out live and direct on Tramspace.

"I'm ordering you to halt this vehicle immediately."

He was addressing the wheelchair-user sitting up at the front where the driver wasn't.

"You what, pal?"

The ex-soldier in the chair was clearly less than impressed.

"I'm telling you to stop this tram. Now."

"And I'm telling you that I'm not the driver. There is no bloody driver."

The tram drew to a halt level with a few people waiting at a bus stop. The policeman stared at us and ten passengers stared right back. It seemed obvious from its demeanour that the tram wasn't going anywhere until the troublemaker left.

When the policeman did finally sod off, I poked through Tramspace. Judging by the amount of similarly-tagged footage, this was not an isolated incident.

* * *

The council began their media campaign that afternoon. We were called eco-terrorists an awful lot. Also troublemakers, irresponsible, fifth columnists, dangerous radicals, and mindless vandals. It didn't help that all their fulminations-to-camera seemed to feature one or more passenger-filled trams trundling along peacefully in the background.

It took a week for them to admit defeat. A week in which the trams became busier as the number of cars clogging up the roads dropped rapidly.

I remembered a story someone had told me at one party or another. He'd been describing what London had been like after a couple of days of the first fuel blockade, how overnight it had become a quiet and pleasantly human-scaled place to be. It was half like that and half like living in one of the *Bristol's Edwardian Past* postcard books.

* * *

My phone chimed as I passed the pub at the end of my road. It was a reminder from the nearest tram that it was five minutes away. The tram helpfully included live feeds from its cameras; the road in front was quiet, but the tram itself was three quarters full. I paged to a view of the tram following a few minutes behind. It was equally busy, so I took the first one.

Half-way to work, another message arrived. This one from Welsh Pete. "Good news," it read. "Pub after work?" I responded in the positive and cc'ed Tramspace so that it would remind me to leave the office in time.

* * *

Pete was waiting for me outside the pub. "Well timed," he said, standing up. "We're to go on up to Brian's, and that tram's just pinged me."

"Any particular reason?" I tried to sound casual.

"He says a mob of suits want to speak to us all."

Compliance. I nodded on autopilot. That lift-shaft feeling was back with a vengeance.

* * *

We assembled around a couple of beer-garden tables in Brian's yard. Besides Pete and Baz, there were two other people that I didn't recognise; a black-clad hacker type who'd taken all his styling clues from Steve Jobs and a power-dressed brunette who appeared determined not to show that she felt out of her depth.

Brian arrived with a cool box, distributed lager, and made introductions. Baz choked on his beer when it turned out that our visitors had come from BMW's advanced research facility.

"We were really impressed with the way you modified our biotech," enthused Tomas, quite obviously the geek being minded by the woman from the legal or PR department.

Their biotech? Compliance never operated on behalf of third parties. Oh, wait. Collaboration cluster.

I glanced at Brian over the end of my bottle and raised an eyebrow. He looked embarrassed but defiant.

"However our legal department"—here Tomas nodded at his minder—"had a sense of humour failure, I think."

Nadine, the brunette, scrunched her face into a what-can-you-do? expression.

"In this sort of case, BMW would vigorously defend its intellectual property rights. However, given the unique nature of the, ah, opportunity here, we have an alternative proposal," she said.

"We're going to open-source the code." Tomas couldn't contain himself. "We'd like to fold in your changes first, then give everyone free access," he beamed at us.

There was a silence. As usual, my mouth started working before my brain had a chance to object.

"But, but...You're the car industry. You build the machines driven by the exact demographic that hates public transport the most. Why are you even talking to us? I mean, I'm sorry and everything, but it's true..." I ground to a halt as Tomas looked speculatively at me and Nadine sighed. They glanced at each other, and she gave him a look that translated as "Go on then. On your own head be it."

"The car as we understand it is at an evolutionary dead end," he said. "Hybrid power plants, biotech-constructed bodies, and drive-by-wire are just staving off the inevitable. Detroit thought they could ignore simple economics, and look what happened to them. You see, management structures are strongly risk-averse, so anyone suggesting that their employer should exit their currently profitable core business is going to find themselves living in interesting times. However, should one be able to arrange an opportunity to, ah, use one's powers for good, it almost becomes a fait accompli."

Brian lurched up out of his chair.

"Fuck," he said.

Tomas raised his eyebrows.

"Yes?"

"It was too easy. The code for the biotech. It wasn't just lying about on an unsecured server, was it?"

Tomas gave a self-deprecating smile. I wanted to smack him.

"It would be wrong of me to comment on that," he said.

"Yes, it would. Unless you want to admit to corporate espionage." The voice came from the yard entrance. Stevens.

Baz stood up. He looked like an angry squaddie.

"Who the hell are you supposed to be?"

"Stevens. Compliance department. That so-called 'unsecured server' is one of ours, isn't it, Ms. Mauriks? It looks like you were better than we thought, and it wasn't quite an inside job after all."

He pointed the approximation of a smile at me.

Tomas turned his smug expression up a notch.

"Well now. This is interesting. So you're the security architect on that system? You really are very good at your job. It took our guy quite a long time to create a convincing hole in your work."

I grimaced. A girl just lives for such compliments.

"Very much were. But thank you."

"In point of fact," Stevens said, "Ms. Mauriks here made an invaluable contribution to our security investigation over the last few weeks."

You bastard.

Baz turned to stare at me.

"Jax? What's this sod on about?"

The words wouldn't come. Stevens beat me to it.

"When we discovered that someone had tampered with our systems, we contacted the original security team. Ms. Mauriks, ah, Jax, was only too pleased to offer assistance in tracking those responsible and monitoring their activities. Thanks to her, I shall be able to make a full report to the audit department tomorrow."

"Jesus, Jax, I thought you were on our side," said Baz.

"Baz, I..."

He gestured angrily with his beer bottle.

"Save it for your friends, girl. Once a suit, always a suit."

"Fuck," said Brian again. He just looked...resigned.

I was feeling sick.

"Come now," said Tomas with near-perfect smackability. "Don't you see that everybody wins? You've grown your quite remarkable transport network, the code for which remains free to use and modify."

"While everyone downloads BMW code and grows BMW trams," I said.

"Exactly."

He leaned forward, forearms on the table, which put his face far too close to mine.

"You provided the most successful viral marketing video in history. You should be very proud."

Pete stood next to Baz and Brian.

"You lot sold us out," he said. It was a statement of fact.

"You idealists with your absolute statements," said Tomas.

I wanted him to go away before I burst into tears. The maddening thing was that he was right; everyone was going to win. It was just on someone else's terms.

I closed my eyes and concentrated hard on my breathing. Tomas stood and carefully placed his mostly-full beer in the centre of the table.

"Now if you'll excuse me, I have a plane to catch."

He strode off out of the yard.

Stevens watched him go, then turned to me.

"Good job, Ms. Mauriks. We'll be in touch."

I didn't watch him leave.

Brian grabbed the cool box and stumped into the furthest-away shed. Pete drained his beer, nudged Baz, and then nodded in Brian's direction. They both went to see if he needed any help getting drunk.

That left me and Nadine. I thought about joining in with the male posturing, but she was picking at the label on her beer and, well, looking quite cute for a lawyer.

"Why are you still here?" I asked.

She looked up, brushed her hands together to remove the incriminating paper scraps, and favoured me with a rueful half smile.

"I, um...Oh, to hell with it. I didn't want to be breathing the same air as that poisonous article. I'll be out of your way as soon as I'm sure he's found a taxi. And, um, I wanted to say that, I mean...Oh god, this sounds stupid. I love Tramspace."

"Oh," I said.

"I think hardware-boy's missed the point. Tramspace is the thing that people play with first and that's the thing they'll expect to be able to use wherever they are, because you don't have to be in Bristol to get a sense of how it works; and that makes it a more open sort of a place when you do get there because you already know how to get around..."

She paused for breath.

"Sorry. That was...Sorry. I think it's safe for me to get out of your way now. Oh. I forgot. I think I have some documents for you."

She dug in her bag and pulled out an A4 envelope. I slid the contents into my hand and flipped through the security documents for the Winchester cluster. It was complete. The paper trail would now show that someone else had come along later and purposely made the system insecure.

"I think I should have given them to you earlier, but I didn't connect the names immediately. Sorry."

"How..?"

"As part of the collaboration agreement, we were provided with a complete system audit. I thought this part might prove useful," said Nadine.

I sat back. I think I'd tensed far too many muscles trying to cope with Tomas and Stevens.

"Thank you," I said. So much for corporate solidarity.

Nadine smiled.

"Not what you expected, right? Look, are there any bars in this city where a girl can get drunk without being pawed at by tedious straight boys?"

I poked at my mobile until I got into the beerfinder add-on for Tramspace. Nadine craned her head to look as the city map scrolled and zoomed, so I dragged my chair sideways and held my phone where we could both easily see it. Of course I knew what the answer would be before beerfinder did, but I was trying to be cool.

"It looks like the top end of Old Market would be best. If you access Tramspace from your mobile it'll tell you which tram to catch and where to get off. Or, um..." I trailed off again.

"Or?" said Nadine.

"Or I could, um, take you there myself. I need more beer after that. I mean, if you want the company."

"Thank you. I'd like that."

My phone chimed.

"Then I think it's time we caught a tram."

After the Change

By Stephanie Burgis

Andrew still remembers the first time it happened: the wings bumping out beneath his stroking fingers, then exploding in thick, white glory from Neve's delicate shoulder blades. The muscles suddenly bulking out her slender arms. Neve's eyes filling with tears and panic.

"What's happening to me?"

He held her through the change and after. She wept in his arms as he looked at the room around them, full of broken furniture and glass.

"We'll figure this out," he promised her. "Together."

He was the one who spent weeks on the Net until he finally found the others, hidden behind password-encoded screens. He was the one who held her hand as she made the phone call, and drove her to the first meeting, at midnight, in the abandoned warehouse behind Temple Meads that the others had taken as their temporary headquarters.

Empty buildings hulked around them in the darkness, left over from a more prosperous decade. The distant rattle of the trains passing through the Temple Meads Nexus mingled with the sound of Neve's quick, shallow breathing.

She clung to his hand as the door opened. A man's wide figure blocked the light from inside, his shoulders freakishly enlarged, bulging with more muscle than any bodybuilder could dream of. He looked at Andrew with eyes that shone golden through narrow slits. "No normals," he growled.

Neve shook her head and backed up, pulling Andrew with her. "I can't do this alone," she whispered to him. "I can't—"

"It's okay," Andrew said, and he nudged her gently forward. "I'll wait outside."

"I don't know—"

"I'll be here when you're ready," he promised. And he was.

But he was the one who wasn't ready when it happened.

* * *

Andrew's waiting up for her tonight. It's four a.m. before he hears the tell-tale creak of the balcony windows opening from outside. He starts up from the couch where he's half-dozed all night long in front of the screen, through ten-year-old wildlife documentaries and re-runs of last night's Prime Minister's Question Time—with David Cameron struggling to answer questions about the rising crime rates and looking as haggard as if each and every demand for a new General Election has added another grey hair to his head.

As Andrew rises to his feet, a two-minute news flash

covers breaking news: the mysterious return of all the paintings and antique Chinese porcelain stolen by a gang of museum robbers two weeks before. All five of the robbers were left on the City Museum steps early this morning, bound and gagged next to proof of their guilt. No one saw the mysterious avengers except one drunken museum guard, who babbled about angels with white wings. The newscaster waggles his eyebrows meaningfully as he passes on that part of the story.

It's only when Andrew flicks off the screen that he hears the voices and realizes Neve isn't alone. All he can hear is a soft male undertone, murmuring something unintelligible.

Andrew's fingers clench into puny, human fists as he walks toward the kitchen. But he keeps his face carefully blank.

"Harris," he says evenly, as he steps into the kitchen he and Neve decorated together, two years ago. "Nice to see you again."

Golden eyes flash at him in quickly veiled anger as the two figures separate. They weren't embracing — not quite — but the image of what he saw is blazoned in Andrew's mind: the two figures leaning into each other as they whispered, Neve's hand clasping her partner's, their wings curved in an intimate arc.

"Andrew," Harris says, and his wings rise to shivering attention above his broad shoulders. "A bit late for you to be up, isn't it? Don't you have a job to go to in just a few hours?"

"Don't you?" Andrew says. "Or is crime-fighting paying all the bills nowadays?"

"Well..." Harris snorts, trades a quick look with Neve.

She hurries toward Andrew, folding her wings behind

her back. Her closed hand slips into the pocket of her shimmering silver stretch-suit; he catches a glimpse of gold chain before it disappears. "Andrew," she says. "What are you doing awake?"

"Waiting for you," Andrew says, and notes every trace of pink on her cheeks.

"I'd better be off then," Harris says. "Good work tonight, Neve."

"Oh, you, too." She turns back toward him, her face lighting up. "That move you did in the gallery was amazing. That guy never knew—"

Harris laughs. "You're just trying to be modest again," he says. "It doesn't work on me, remember? You know you saved my life at least twice tonight."

"Oh, no, not really, only—"

"Goodnight, then," Andrew says loudly, and the two of them jump apart.

"Andrew," Harris says and jerks his square chin in a nod. His golden eyes soften as he turns toward the balcony windows, wings preparing for flight. "See you tonight, Neve."

"Tonight," she repeats, and smiles until the windows close behind him. Then she swings on Andrew, her brows furrowing. "What's wrong with you? You were so rude—"

"You're going out again tonight?" Andrew says. "You've been out every night this week."

"I have to," she says. "What we've figured out—the clues we found tonight, and earlier this week—we think there's someone behind all these crazy local crime figures, someone with a plan. So—"

"If you took one night off, would the city collapse?" Andrew asks. "Before you changed—"

"But that's why it happened! Don't you see?" Her eyes

brighten with enthusiasm. "Harris figured it out. So many of us changing, all at once—it has to be the city itself calling us into being. With so much new crime, so much danger, the city needs us—"

"Harris figured that out, did he?" Andrew says. "Right. Well, no point arguing, then, is there?" He turns back toward the living room, his vision blurring.

If Neve punched the cupboard, it would collapse, shattering plates and cups across the room. If Harris did, the whole kitchen might explode. If Andrew tried, only his hand would hurt. And he can't bear to let her see that. Not tonight. Not anymore.

"Andrew —" Neve begins.

"Forget it," he says and heads for the bedroom before he can lose control completely. "Harris was right. As usual. It's too late for normals like me to be awake."

* * *

Andrew's head throbs dully throughout breakfast, three hours later. He drinks his coffee and stares into space, too tired to think. Neve rustles nearby, making her own breakfast. He feels her nervous gaze flick across him. He doesn't turn to meet her eyes. He doesn't want to see the worry in them...or the pity.

When they first moved in together, they used to listen to music at breakfast. His 80s metal collection met her alternative punk, Metallica clashing with Ani DiFranco. They took turns every morning, and made outrageous fun of each other's choices. Once Neve shrieked so loudly in outrage at one of his insults, Andrew pretended to fall off his chair in shock, and she fell down right on top of him onto the tiled floor, their legs and arms tangling, his laughter muffled by her long, red hair, her laughter warm against his shoulder.

The clock in the corner of the kitchen ticks away seconds, the only soundtrack to their meal.

"We caught some robbers last night," Neve says as she sits down across the table, looking up at him through lowered eyelashes. Her wings are furled so tightly behind her back, he can barely see them. "They'd broken into the art gallery in the City Museum and—"

"I know," Andrew says. "I saw it on the news."

"Oh." She lifts a spoonful of Weetabix to her lips, stares at it, and sets it back down in the bowl. "I was the one who figured out where they were hiding. It was really..." Her voice trails off.

Andrew eats a bite of toast, not tasting it.

She says, "You could—"

"What?" Andrew says. "What could I do?" The dry toast crumbles in his grip. "What could I possibly do, Neve?"

"I don't know!" She sets her spoon on the table, her hands shaking. "You could stop being such an arsehole. You could start acting normal again. You could—"

"I am normal," Andrew says. "Remember? That's the problem."

"It's not a problem, it's just..." She hisses breath through her teeth. "Why are you so angry all the time?"

"How would you know how I feel?" Andrew says. "When are you ever here to see it?"

"I'm here now," Neve says. "So tell me."

"Stay home tonight," Andrew says. "If you actually care."

She closes her eyes. "I can't. I promised Harris—"

"Right," Andrew says. "Harris. Because that's all that

matters now, isn't it?"

"That's not true." Neve's fists clench around the edges of the table. Andrew hears an ominous creaking sound from the straining wood. "I don't understand why this is so hard for you. You were there for my Change. You know how important this is to me. You know—"

"I was there," Andrew says. "But you aren't here anymore, are you? Not really."

"Don't be ridiculous!" Neve says. "Look, Harris says normals just can't understand and I shouldn't even hope for anything different, but I know you and I know—"

"That's it," Andrew says and stands up, scattering toast crumbs. "Why don't you go ahead and have the rest of this conversation with Harris, like you really want to? He's the only one you listen to nowadays."

Wood snaps. Neve's half of the table breaks off into her lap, spilling milk and china and silverware. Her cereal bowl shatters on the floor. She leaps to her feet, covered in milky chunks of Weetabix. Andrew's chest tightens at the sight.

"Neve," he says, "I'm s—"

The balcony windows explode into the room, showering glass. Andrew flings his arms up before his face. Shards bite into his skin as he lunges forward to pull Neve out of danger.

Black-clad men tumble through the broken windows, head over heels, in a smooth, curving arc through the air. Neve whirls to confront them, her fists rising to a fighting stance, her wings billowing out like thick, white shields between Andrew and the intruders.

"Run!" she yells.

"What the hell—?" Andrew starts.

A black dart arcs through the air and buries itself in

Neve's neck. Her eyes widen. Then her head falls back and she crumples to the ground. Her wings splay across the floor, twisted and limp.

Time goes still. A wordless bellow is coming out of Andrew's mouth. He feels himself moving slowly, so slowly through the air toward her attackers—

And then everything goes black.

When he wakes up on the floor an hour later, surrounded by shattered glass, his skin is bleeding from a dozen places. The windows gape open above him, letting in a cool breeze from the docks and the comforting engine sounds of a water bus passing outside. The clock ticks in the corner.

Neve is gone.

* * *

Gone.

Andrew's head is empty.

Gone.

He stares out the broken windows. The sun is bright overhead.

Gone.

He turns and runs for the phone in the living room.

Of course, he doesn't know the new number. Damn it! He doesn't know any of their numbers. They all change every few weeks, for safety's sake, just like their headquarters move across the city, never staying in the same place for more than a month. He stares at the cordless phone in his hands and watches it shake. It's only then that he realizes he's trembling.

If he'd asked Neve, she would have told him how to contact the others. She used to, in the beginning, back when she told him everything. But then he stopped wanting to know.

Gone.

The black dart buried in her neck...

The phone falls to the ground by his feet. The room whirls around him.

He throws out a hand to steady himself. *Neve's Blackberry.* The numbers will be there.

Andrew chants the two words to himself like a mantra all the way across the living room, into the bedroom. He digs through her purse, past lipstick and receipts, tissues and tampons. *Neve's Blackberry,* he tells himself reassuringly, but the back of his head sounds an echoing counterpoint: *Gone, gone, gone...*

He pulls the Blackberry out. There are two new messages, both from Harris. The first one says:

Call me when he's gone.

The second one says: *Get out now.*

* * *

Andrew tries three different ways of phrasing his message. Finally he gives up and just writes the bare truth. *They took Neve,* he types. Then, gritting his teeth, he gives in and begs: *Please tell me what's happening. Tell me what I can do.*

He waits for hours. But there is no reply.

* * *

The phone sits silent on its hook all through the morning and afternoon. Andrew sits in front of it, on the living room carpet. The bleeding cuts on his arms and face

56

and feet gradually slow and dry. Through the lace curtains, he watches the light shift outside, listens to the cries of the seagulls. Neve's Blackberry sits on his lap. He checks it every five minutes, just in case.

There's someone, a single person, behind Bristol's rising crime rates. He remembers that much from last night's discussion. But who is it? Neve talked about finding clues. But there are no clues hidden in her Blackberry. Nothing but carefully coded messages from Harris that Andrew can't even begin to understand. But that's the point, isn't it? Normals aren't supposed to understand. Only the city's Chosen.

And outside the flat, the city is moving, undisturbed, in its daily business, water buses and sailing boats sweeping through the harbour, students canoeing, pubs serving customers, the new tram system finally being built. No one has come to a standstill except for Andrew. The city that Changed Neve to fight its battles doesn't care that she's been kidnapped. And Andrew doesn't know how to save her.

At eight o'clock that night, the phone rings. He lunges for it, barely thinking by then, barely capable of it.

A man's voice hisses down the phone.

"Bring it to me tonight if you want to see her alive."

" 'It'?" Andrew says. But the word chokes on his dry throat, comes out as just a cough. He swallows hard and tries again. "Where is she? Where—"

"The warehouse," the voice hisses. "Be there in an hour." There's a click on the other end of the line, and then only a dial tone sounds in Andrew's ear.

He lowers the phone. " 'It'?" he says. " 'It'?" he repeats to the empty air. "What the fuck is 'it,' Neve?" he bellows.

The faint sound of the dial tone is his only answer. He

pulls out Neve's Blackberry, checks it again. Still no reply from Harris. He types a second message: *Call me now. I need to know what they want!*

Outside, he hears a car horn honk and the jingle of a bicyclist's bell. The sky through the windows is dark, not quite black.

The warehouse is half an hour's drive away.

Andrew lunges into the bedroom, turns Neve's purse upside down. But there's nothing there that he hasn't seen before, nothing special. He checks his watch. Twenty-five minutes until he has to leave. He searches her desk in the corner of the room, pillaging the drawers, scattering papers across the floor. Street maps of Bristol covered by black-inked notes in Neve's small, precise handwriting. Print-outs of "Most Wanted" posters. Newspaper articles about local crimes.

Fifteen minutes.

He turns, stares wildly across the room. Neve's shining, silver suit hangs neatly in the open closet, winking at him in the half-darkness. He's across the room a moment later, with no memory of how he got there. His hands are buried in the shimmering silver fabric, pressing it against his face. It smells of Neve: her perfume, and her sweat. She fought in it last night. It's here. Why isn't she?

She tried to tell him who she fought. She tried to tell him...

His shoulders are heaving. Dry, racking sobs tear through his throat. The silver fabric presses against his face, smoother than silk but tougher than steel. Neve was so proud of it when she first brought it home. She put it on and pirouetted for him, her wings sweeping out behind her, and he...

Andrew draws back, gasping for breath, pulling away

from the memories. The fabric...

He looks again at the fabric between his fingers. So smooth, and yet so tough. Like no other fabric he's ever seen or felt before...

He looks at his watch. Two minutes left.

"I'm sorry, Neve," he whispers. "I fucked up."

He pulls the suit off its hanger. It's the only magical thing in this room, the only beautiful, special oddity left in the whole house. The only remnant of Neve.

He carries it tucked up against him like a baby all the way out to the car park.

* * *

Andrew pulls up in front of the warehouse twenty-six minutes later. Last time he came here, for Neve's first meeting, he circled the area for almost ten minutes until he found a parking space that looked almost safe, two blocks away. This time he drags the car to a shuddering halt directly in front of the main doors, veering across double yellow lines.

The doors are closed. The building looks dark and empty. Deserted. It looked that way last time, too.

He turns the key in the ignition and puts it in his pocket. "Here goes nothing," he whispers.

Andrew picks up the shimmering silver suit from the passenger seat. As he picks it up, something bumps against his hand. He can feel something small, something hidden—it's in Neve's pocket. He reaches inside and draws out a long, slender golden chain. A pendant hangs from it: a linked pair of golden wings, small, romantic, and oddly wistful against the chain's glittering loveliness.

It's the chain he saw her slipping into her pocket last

night. The jewellery Harris had given her.

His hands clench around it. For a moment, the old panic rises within him to shoulder aside the new, almost blinding him. The jewellery Harris gave her, that she hid before Andrew could see it...Was she waiting to put it on until Andrew left for work today? Until —

Andrew shakes his head sharply, pushing aside the tidal wave of emotions. When he gets Neve back...

His breath hurts. His head is suddenly resting against the steering wheel, pressed hard against the safe, cool, artificial normality of the rubber wheel, as if he could soak it in and absorb it, make his whole life normal again. But he forces his thought through to its conclusion anyway. *If he gets Neve back, he'll ask her about the necklace. But he can't afford to worry about that now.*

He sits up and slips it into the pocket of his jeans. The slender chain curls into a surprisingly warm weight against his thigh. It feels oddly comforting there, despite everything: a reminder of Neve, in all her secrets and mystery.

He opens the car door, and the massive doors to the warehouse swing open in front of him. Carrying the silver suit in his arms, Andrew steps into darkness.

The doors slam shut behind him. Light flashes down the corridor like an arrow, pointing to a further set of doors fifty feet away.

The smooth, shimmering fabric of Neve's suit brushes against Andrew's arms as he walks down the corridor. Neve's necklace is a small, centering point of warmth against his thigh.

Almost there, he chants silently. *Almost there...*

He pushes the doors open and steps into a fever-dream.

This room of the warehouse must have held millions of crates once. Now the great, echoing space is full of colour and motion and impossibilities. Silver machines whir in the corners, creating weapons that glitter and shine as they fall into piles on the ground. An enormous tank of water takes up the whole back half of the room, filled with flashing, lethal shapes and hunks of bloody meat. A man— a creature—sits high above it all, in a grotesquely ornate throne raised six feet above the ground. And on the floor before him—

"Neve!" Andrew says, and breaks into a run.

"Stop," says the man on the throne, and six black-clad guards step forward to point their dart guns straight at Andrew.

He drags to a reluctant halt, but he's still not looking at them or at the man who sits above them. His eyes are on Neve, bound in chains, kneeling at the bottom of the steps that lead up to the throne. Her blue eyes widen with panic as she stares at him. Marks of tears show on her pale face, and her short, red hair sticks out at odd, matted angles, as if hunks of it have been ripped out. Her beautiful, white wings are distorted by the angle of the heavy chains that bind them; he can see blood seeping down the feathers.

"Let her go!" he says. "I brought it, just like you said. So—"

"Andrew, no!" Neve struggles to rise to her feet, trips on her own chains, and falls back to her knees. "Don't give it to him! Don't—"

"If you do not give it to me," the man above her says with calm precision, "I will kill her just as I've already killed two of her colleagues, and then I will make you wish I had killed you as well. Do you understand me?"

For the first time, Andrew looks up at the man, whose

voice he recognizes from the phone. He sees the glittering golden eyes he knows from Harris and the other men who have Changed, the bulging, muscled shoulders, the wings...but the wings are covered with a faint yellow sheen, and even the golden eyes look wrong—almost painted on. He blinks and looks again.

The man's lips curve into a thin smile. "Impressed?" he says. "You should be." He holds out his hand. "Bring it to me."

Andrew swallows hard and holds the other man's distorted golden gaze. "First let Neve go," he says.

The man laughs. "I don't think so. If she—"

"Let her go," Andrew says. "I'll stay here until you're satisfied I've brought exactly what you wanted. Just let her go free first."

"Andrew—" Neve starts, in a choked voice he barely recognizes.

But the man above them talks straight across her. "Very brave and heroic," he says. "And yet somehow, also, incredibly suspicious." He snaps his fingers. "I want to see what you've brought me, now. And if you've been lying to me, I will kill her in front of you and then torture you until you tell me where it really is." The words themselves are unreal, unbelievable, but his voice is flat, and conviction sounds in every word.

This isn't real life. This isn't Andrew's life. But Neve is kneeling, bound, in front of him, and he couldn't walk away even if the guards would let him.

"Fine," Andrew says, and his voice doesn't waver. He walks past Neve, up the broad steps that lead to the ridiculously overblown throne that belongs on a Hollywood movie set, or in a nightmare. He passes Neve's silver suit into the other man's huge, powerful hands.

"Here it is," Andrew says. "Now let her go."

The man frowns. He turns the suit over. He pats it down. He shakes it above his lap. And then, for the first time, Andrew sees real emotion on his face, as his painted-yellow eyes widen, first in shock and then in outrage.

"You thought you could trick me?" he breathes. His voice rises to a bellow—nearly a shriek. "You thought you could make a fool out of me and get away with it? You're just like them! Coming into my city, ruining everything, trying to take over as if I were nothing, as if they could just shove all my work aside—" Flecks of spit fly out of his mouth, scattering through the air as he rises from the throne to loom over Andrew.

"What did you expect me to do?" Andrew shouts back. "You didn't tell me what to bring! All you said was bring 'it'! How the hell was I supposed to know what 'it' was? You think she tells me what they're doing? You think I'm one of them? You think—"

"The necklace, you idiot!" the other man bellows. And at Andrew's sudden, wide-eyed freeze, he finally relaxes. His lips curve into a smile; he sinks back into his seat. "Aha. You have seen it, at least."

"I..." Andrew swallows, licks dry lips. "I thought..."

"She didn't tell you what it does?" The other man shakes his head. "Her own partner. She could have saved you, did you know that? Could have made you just like her. But she chose not to."

"What are you talking about?" Andrew breaks the other man's gaze, turns to look down at Neve at the bottom of the steps. But she doesn't speak. She only bites her lip, her face pale. He swings back to the other man. "What do you mean?"

"It's a miracle," the other man says. "A genuine

miracle, and they stole it away from me to keep all the power to themselves, because they couldn't bear to share it with the rest of us. It Changes people."

"But that—the Change, it just happens, it just—"

"It just happened to them," the man says softly, "but now it can happen to us, too, if we want it. You see me, don't you? The necklace works. You can be one of them, too. Just like her."

Andrew stares back at him. His chest is tight with pressure; the golden chain throbs against his thigh, through the fabric of his jeans.

"She was never going to tell you," the other man says softly. "But I will. And I'll let you use it, too. You'll never be left behind again."

"It's true," Neve says. Her voice sounds wrong, muffled with strain.

Andrew turns slowly to look back at her. Her blue eyes are fierce with intensity. He knows that look; at least, he did know it, once.

"All he needs to do is put it on," she says clearly. "That's all he needs to do."

Andrew reaches into his jeans pocket. The golden chain tingles with warmth against his fingers. The man in front of him leans so close they're almost touching, head to head.

"Yes," he breathes. "You can put it on, if you like, before you give it to me. I understand you, you know. I'm the only one who can."

Andrew draws the necklace from his pocket; stretches the chain out into a long, looping oval; stares at the tiny, glittering, golden wings, wistful and perfect as they dangle in mid-air before him.

"All right," he says. "I will put it on."

He lunges forward and throws the chain over the other man's head.

The man's shriek pierces the air. Andrew stumbles backward down the steps. The other man's body is twisting, warping above the ornate throne. He flails blindly, his eyes squeezed shut in pain. Guards come flying across the room, but none of them attacks. They're too busy staring at their leader, gabbling in agitation.

Andrew grabs for Neve, pulls at the chains. They won't budge. He tries to pull her to her feet, but the heavy chains hold her down. The other man's screams rise higher and higher.

"Thank you," Neve says. "Thank you so much. Now run!"

"I'm not running."

"There's nothing more you can do—" she begins. And then the doors burst open behind Andrew, and her face lights up. "Harris!"

Harris is a blur of energy lunging toward them, knocking guards aside. He takes in the situation with a look, shoulders Andrew aside so hard Andrew falls to the floor, and kneels down beside Neve to rip the chains off her.

Andrew lies on his back on the warehouse floor, adrift. The high, grey roof above him is obscured by the yellow-white feathers that fill the air, showering from the top of the golden throne, falling onto Andrew and the floor beside him. The other man's wings are coming off, but not easily. Blood mixes with the feathers. The man screams and screams as his body warps and shrinks. Andrew cannot look away.

"Good work," he hears Harris say to Neve. "How did you get the necklace back on him?"

"I didn't," Neve says. "It was Andrew."

"Huh." There's a moment of silence. Then Harris says to Andrew, "Well done."

Andrew hunches a shoulder and turns away from them.

The man atop the throne is a shrunken, pallid creature. His eyes are brown, only streaked by yellow now. His back is bleeding. He clutches his narrow shoulders, huddles in upon his thin, helpless body. His eyes fix on Andrew's watching face, and he pulls off the necklace. He tosses it down the steps with a snarl. Then he turns and leaps straight from the high throne into the tank of water.

Flashing shapes descend upon him. His screams are drowned.

Andrew shakes and shakes.

Neve is suddenly beside him, helping him to his feet, murmuring something he can't catch through the memory of the other man's screams, still ringing in his ears. Harris leans down to scoop up the glittering necklace from the steps.

"Time to get rid of this," he says. "I'm not sure how to destroy it, but if we—"

"Wait," Neve says.

"What?" Harris looks between them. His golden eyes widen. "Neve, no. We agreed on this. You were the one who said we couldn't—"

"I don't care," Neve says. "Andrew." She forces him to meet her gaze. "Do you want to put on the necklace?"

"Neve—"

"Shut up, Harris!" She puts both hands around Andrew's face, her slim fingers cool against his cheeks. "You can do it. It's okay."

Andrew stares at her. "It destroyed him."

"That was because it Changed him back when he wore it again. All you have to do is take care never to put it on again, and—"

"No," Andrew said. "That isn't what I meant." He steps back, letting her hands fall away from him. Takes another step back, and then another, until he's facing them both. "I wasn't chosen by the city," he says.

"That doesn't matter! We have the necklace, we can make you—"

"I wasn't chosen," Andrew repeats. "And I think there was a reason."

"But..." Neve stares at him, tears in her eyes. "What are you saying?"

"I'm saying I can't do this," Andrew says. "I'm sorry, Neve."

* * *

They walk out of the warehouse together, all three of them. The guards are safely tied up inside; Neve and Harris saw to that. The police have been alerted, and they'll be here soon to clean up the bodies, the living and the dead; to cart away the empty golden throne.

Andrew's car is still parked, skew-angled, against the kerb. He stops in front of it, so tired he can barely move. The closest street lamp is half a block away, casting just enough light to make out the handle of the door. He wonders how he'll manage to drive home. He wonders if it would be better just to sleep at the wheel. Maybe forever.

Harris looks at him, looks away, and finally speaks. "Look," he says, his voice a low rumble. "I'm sorry I didn't answer your messages today."

Andrew shrugs. There's nothing he can say.

"What messages?" Neve says.

"It doesn't matter—" Andrew starts, but Harris cuts across him.

"I should have answered," he said. "But I didn't think there was anything you could do. So I didn't bother."

Andrew shrugs again, heavily. "Forget it," he says. "It all worked out in the end." He takes hold of the door handle with his left hand, hanging on to the top of the car with his other hand to hold himself upright. "Anyway," he says. "I'll see you. Both of you."

He opens the door and takes a deep breath, preparing himself for the long slide into the driver's seat, the longer drive back to the empty house afterwards. He hears the scuffling of feet behind him. Then Neve says, "Wait."

Andrew waits. He doesn't move. He's still staring into the dark, empty car. He can't look away, or he'll never manage what he needs to do.

"Can I come with you?" Neve says.

He turns. The motion seems to take forever.

Her blue eyes are shadowed in the faint light of the street lamp. Her red hair sticks out at odd angles. Her wings are unfurled, white and perfect behind her. Harris stands a few feet behind her in the darkness, turned half-away. With a lurch of reluctant empathy, Andrew recognises the expression on the other man's face.

"You don't have to," he says, speaking to both of them now. "It's okay. You've moved on. I can see that. So you don't need to pretend—"

"I don't want to move on without you," Neve says. "I thought I might have to, but—" She pauses, swallowing visibly; tries to smile. It doesn't work. "I want to move on together."

It feels too dangerous to hold her gaze, too unbearable to look away. "Everything's different now," he says.

"We were always different. Don't you remember?"

"But I'm not..." Andrew's voice trails off. He's looking into her blue eyes and remembering a hundred arguments and a hundred reconciliations. A hundred different songs and a hundred different lovemakings. Both kinds of music, mingling into one.

"Yes," he says. "God, yes. Please."

"Well, then." Neve smiles again, and this time it's real—not the smile he used to know, free and confident, but a new one, fierce with determination and relief. He can feel its mirror image on his own lips. He's barely aware of Harris moving away from them with slow, unhappy steps.

Neve puts her small, strong hand on his. She could crush his fingers if she squeezed too hard, but her touch is as light as a feather. "Give me the keys and shift over," she says. "I'm driving us home."

A Tale of Two Cities

By Christina Lake

"It was the best of times, it was the worst of times," I began. No one reads Charles Dickens any more, so I thought I could get away with it. "It was the age of the Internet, it was the age of Aquarius, it was an epoch of waste, and an epoch of high environmental principles. It was a season of darkest terror and a season of brightest freedom."

That's the point where my sister would usually say: "Get on with it, Syd!" But my audience, a delegation from one of the new fractal nations, was respectful. Maybe they really wanted to hear what life had been like back in 21st century Bristol?

"In those days, Bristol was a city of two halves," I said, "split down the middle by a great road where the M32 building now stands and divided politically by the battle between those who still loved their motor cars and those who wanted to ban them. Petrol was running out, and while the rich could buy vehicles that ran on other fuels, the poor still queued up for their ration. The Bristol First party had just defeated the old political parties in the local elections and was determined to make the city one of the wealthiest and most prestigious in the country. Their only opposition came from the eco-activists who still dreamed of a carbon-neutral Bristol."

The fractals nodded dutifully, even though they probably knew all this from their own research. There were six of them, dressed in last year's fashion (or was it last decade's?) of kaftans and baggy trousers, although the woollen hats and dreadlocks were unique to them. It struck me that they must be plugged into some network of their own, sharing thoughts, as they had the distracted look of people tracking several narratives at once. I decided to move on to my part of the story, the story I'd learned from my mother about the day their forebears lost St. Paul's and how I came to be who I was.

* * *

It was Avatar Friday in the office and my mother, Hannah, was bored. Everyone else was working from home—even the robots on reception were actual 'bots, programmed to recite company slogans about protecting and conserving water every time someone stepped through the door.

The only other living person in the building was my namesake Syd, clerk to the company solicitor. Hannah was a bit afraid of Syd. He had a sarcastic manner, and she was fairly sure he was an alcoholic. In those days it was perfectly acceptable to boast about how much you could drink. But Syd didn't boast, he just turned up to work with unsteady hands and the whiff of booze and mints on his breath, and that, quite definitely, was not all right.

Hannah was in the office that day, only because she'd arranged a rendezvous with the company solicitor, Syd's boss Tony. Or, to put it another way, my mum was having an affair with my dad.

Hannah knew she should hate herself for dating a married man. It had begun, as such things do, at the Christmas party. Then there'd been a business trip to France, stolen afternoons at her flat, sex in his office. It was all so clichéd. And now she was going to hit him with the biggest cliché of all.

Or so she'd thought. But on that particular Friday, there was no Tony, real or virtual, in the office. Hannah had been stood up.

My mother would have sloped off home, except that she, or rather her Avatar, was supposed to be at a meeting.

* * *

"Avatars were purely digital in those days," I explained, noticing that some of the delegates looked confused. I wondered if any of them were Avatars themselves. Nowadays it's difficult to tell, but this bunch from way out in the suburbs didn't look rich enough to own such state-of-the-art toys. "And there weren't any implants either," I added. "Everybody had to manipulate their Avatars physically, using consoles and keypads."

The two youngest delegates, a boy and girl barely at the age of citizenship, looked sceptical, and I could hardly blame them. They'd probably had their first implant before they could talk, and would find it impossible to function without them.

* * *

So there was Hannah, stuck at her computer, when much to her delight the virtual office—with its virtual meeting space and virtual speakers—disappeared from the screen. After ten minutes of dead air, Hannah was ready to decamp when a priority call hit her desk. It was from Valèry Evrémonde, owner of their French parent company.

My mother had never spoken to Evrémonde before, and was not sure what to expect. He had a reputation for arrogant brilliance. After all, he was the kind of crazy maverick who'd pumped water from the Camargue to Cannes just so the film festival could go ahead. Hannah'd heard other stuff too, rumours about what went on in the company's labs in Lyons, weird experiments and the like, but she didn't really believe them.

Evrémonde, suave in designer casual jacket, was all charm and menace. "Where is everyone?" he asked. "I need to speak to my niece."

Charley Evrémonde had been running the Bristol end of the Evrémonde business empire for the last eighteen months, picking up the pieces, or some might say, master-minding the cover-up, after an unfortunate water pollution incident had led to the death of a child, and the near-prosecution of the whole management team.

"I don't think Charley's in today," said Hannah, hesitating under the impact of Evrémonde's attention. He looked pretty good for someone in his late fifties, but there was something unsettling about his smile, which failed to hide the force of his will.

"Find her, wherever she is," said Evrémonde. "Tell her a potentially harmful chemical's been detected in the supply, so she'd better cut the water to St. Paul's and Easton, before there's trouble."

"What chemical?" asked Hannah. "I'm a Senior Water Protection Officer, it's my job to..."

"The labs'll send over the analysis," Evrémonde interrupted. In his tower room in Lyons he said to someone she couldn't see: "Bon dieu, c'est le formule pour le Qartazine"

"What's Qartazine?" my mother dared to ask. She knew by heart every chemical they used in water treatment, but she'd never heard of that one.

"It's unimportant. I'll send the details to Charley. Your job is to find her, understand?"

"Okay," said Hannah, "but it might take a while with the office off-line."

"Just do it," he said. "I'm sure you can." He smiled his predator's smile. "Hannah. That's your name, isn't it?"

My mother didn't relish her new commission. She disliked Charley Evrémonde for being beautiful, rich, and in charge, and for the extra reason that she was rumoured to have had an affair with Tony. But there was no choice— Hannah had to find Charley, wherever she was. My mother set the reception robots to ring all known numbers for Charley, while she tried the control centre and the emergency hotline; but nobody, it seemed, knew where Charley was.

* * *

"So where was she?" asked one of the men in my audience. He was darker than the rest, and looked muscular under his kaftan, as if he still cared about his body. As if he thought he might want to go on using it after its first youth was gone. There was a spark about him that you don't see too often these days.

74

"Ah, that's where it gets interesting," I said. "Charley Evrémonde wasn't in the office because she was planning on leaving the country with my sister Lucie. Which was why she'd arranged for the virtual office to go offline, so no one would notice she'd gone — least of all her uncle."

My sister prefers to keep her name out of the news these days, but I was still expecting these amateur researchers to wonder what rich, successful, nepotistically-endowed Charley Evrémonde had to do with my infant sister Lucie. After all, Charley wasn't Lucie's mother, but thanks to technology developed in secret in the Evrémonde lab, and that very same drug Quartazine, or QweeZee as they called it on the streets, she had a closer relationship with my sister than any mother.

Well, almost any mother.

But the big man was silent; probably warned not to interrupt by their leader, a slim, androgynous-looking woman standing next to him. These fractals run tight control on their citizens, even if they are only a small community. I decided to press on with the story.

"Imagine, if you please," I said, "Charley Evrémonde walking across the grassy open spaces of the Downs, blown along by the winds of climate change, past an old water tower, and on into Clifton. Heading to a house where busy executives left their children to enjoy the purity of the air and the safety of the controlled access neighbourhood."

"Why wasn't Charley in her car?" asked one of the younger delegates. "I thought you said the rich people all loved their cars."

"They did, but no one was allowed to drive cars in a protected area like Clifton outside rush hour. All the residences had little electric scooters to get around on."

"What, like children?" he asked.

"No, these scooters were solid, heavy things that didn't leave the ground."

I could sense the leader's impatience at these irrelevant details and decided to hurry on. "The point was no one could enter the district without a valid ID card. Charley's card was programmed to let her into those quiet, privileged suburban streets, with their stone mansions, which even she couldn't afford, despite her uncle's largesse. By contrast, my father Tony's ID card, successful lawyer though he was, shouldn't have gained him admittance, for he had no legitimate business in the area.

"But Tony's card, like his identity, was a fake, and he was already there, waiting for Charley."

* * *

My mother, of course, had no idea that Tony was in Clifton waiting for Charley—but she did have instincts. And her instincts told her that two people going off radar at the same time might be more than a coincidence.

So, Hannah found herself obliged to suppress her embarrassment and go and talk to Syd, the office drunk. Syd, who knew about her affair with Tony. Syd, who'd covered for them when they were out of the office, and attended virtual meetings on Tony's behalf (and, occasionally, on hers).

Syd was slumped at his desk in the corner of my father's office, half-hidden behind a pile of books, his suit crumpled as if he'd been out on the town all night. The dark stubble on his face made him look like a cartoon gangster.

"I need to get hold of Tony," said my mother. "It's an emergency." She found it hard to meet Syd's eyes, which — although bloodshot—were alert and slightly creepy.

"Tony's out with a client," said Syd. "What's the emergency?"

"Well, the whole office is down in case you hadn't noticed."

Syd pointed to his desk. "That's why we still have books. Technically obsolete, maybe, but far more stable than your actual pixels."

"And the Director General wants me to find Charley and tell her to cut off the water to Easton and St Paul's."

"So? Isn't that what you people do in Water Protection?"

Hannah started to get angry. "It's not my job to make that kind of decision. He wants to talk to Charley right away."

"Mlle Evrémonde, no doubt, has better things to do with 'Le Weekend' than wait around at the beck and call of her uncle. Here's a suggestion. Tell Evrémonde she's unavailable and let him sort out this crisis and earn his salary."

Syd was good at keeping secrets because nobody paid much attention to him, especially when my father was around. But Hannah had no one else in the office to look at, and suddenly it seemed to her that this debauched and slovenly man was behaving a touch too calmly. Syd knew something, and her guess was that it was something to do with Tony, and with Charley Evrémonde.

"Just put me through to Tony," she said. "I know you know where he is."

Syd shook his head. He was loyal to Tony. Too loyal.

My mother sighed in frustration. "Do you know what Qartazine is?"

Syd's rat-like eyes took on an expression of fascinated horror. "Oh dear, oh dear," he said. "You're really in trouble now."

* * *

I could tell I had my audience hooked. Their faces, all so similar, looked up at me agog, their skin honey brown, genetically homogenised by the neo-Darwinist forces of fashion, politics, and the job market.

Seeing as these delegates of our local fractal nation were so interested, I decided to offer them some extra insight into the street life of old-time Bristol: "My subject was a typical 21st century boy, yet he could just as easily have been around in Dickens's day, a dispossessed orphan lad, perhaps, taken in by the soft-hearted heroine of Dickens's great unwritten novel about the West Country. But this boy wasn't an orphan. His dad was in the army. Or maybe he'd left town for a job in Poland. The stories varied. In any case, the boy's earliest memories were of drinking cider out on the street with his mother.

"Those were happy days," I told my listeners. "Our little boy slept out under the stars with his dogs to keep him warm, lulled asleep by the sound of the traffic. Sharing food with his mother's friends. All that food that people used to throw away; every day more than you would eat in a week, so the boy never went hungry. But sometimes, even with the dogs, they were cold because the winds then were fiercer than now, and the snow came at any time of year, sleeting through the streets in sudden storms. And no one would take them indoors and offer them a bed because they said that was the council's job. But the boy's mother didn't trust the council, and they stayed out on the streets whatever the weather."

"Not in St Paul's," insisted their researcher, the one who had sent me the history they were writing. "We were a hospitable community. We wouldn't leave a woman and her child out on the streets." The researcher was young and intense. The strain in her voice suggested she was channelling views from the rest of the fractal community.

"There were a lot of people out on the street all round the city," I said. "You just looked after your own." That was the way it was, but I could tell it wasn't what she wanted to hear.

"One day," I continued, "the mother was arrested for stealing, and her son was taken away and sent to live with a family in a synthetic house on the edge of the city. He slept alone in a tiny bedroom, with walls so thin he couldn't sneeze without someone complaining. The streets in that part of town were always empty, and he wasn't even allowed a dog.

"Which was why, when he was old enough, he went to live on the bridge. Not the famous bridge that all the tourists go to see, but a footbridge over that motorway road, which separated the two halves of the city—the complacent North from the aspiring South, the middle-class bohemians from the drug-fuelled, no-go zones. At least that's what his friend Tony used to tell him when he brought him a coffee, or dropped some change into his hat.

"The bridge was built out of cheap materials, prefabricated metal, concrete and lumpy tarmac. It smelled of petrol fumes, and dank, stale water and was so narrow that it swayed in the wind or when a heavy lorry passed underneath it. People would meet on the bridge to hand each other packages. Muggers would lurk there, waiting for unwary rich kids out for a night in the rough part of town. Or maybe they weren't muggers, Tony said, but undercover cops trying to bust drug gangs. Tony himself met people there, crop-headed activists on bikes, all convinced they could change the world. The bridge was a magnet for those who wanted to avoid the checkpoints that controlled the traffic between the two parts of the city, a handy route for dropouts, criminals, and anyone else without an ID card.

"But our Dickensian hero didn't mind that. He enjoyed the activity of the bridge. It felt homely. He could smell the cider on the breath of his new friends and hear the comforting drone of traffic passing underneath him as he went to sleep every night."

No one had interrupted, but I sensed a slight impatience, as if they were eager to rejoin Charley as she was blown down the street towards the crèche, and towards my father.

* * *

Charley didn't see Tony until it was too late because her hair, always so chic and well-behaved in the office, was blowing across her face and into her eyes.

He was there and she was there, and there was no avoiding him.

"Why are you taking my daughter out of the country?" asked Tony.

"I'm not." Cold denial, she found, worked with most people.

"Don't play the innocent. I've seen the flight bookings."

This was bad. Charley had thought her bookings were a secret. But now Tony knew she would have to invent a story to convince him to let her leave. "The little girl I've come to pick up isn't your daughter, Tony, I swear. My uncle lied to you. He altered the pictures to make her look like your daughter. But really she's my daughter by a man back in France."

Charley realised that Tony would know the truth as soon as he saw the girl. He would recognise her eyes, her dark hair, and her bone-structure, and all the other features that Charley's uncle had cloned so successfully. For Valèry Evrémonde's ambitions were not to be satisfied through rearranging the waterways of France, or appearing onscreen with movie stars; in his lab in France he was experimenting on the stuff of life itself, DNA, and the encoding of consciousness.

"If she's really your daughter, why are you running away to America with her?" asked Tony. "You've just spent a fortune on a visa and a Green Card, all without telling your uncle."

"Because I hate my uncle," said Charley. This at least was true. "Why should I use my daughter to keep you working for him? He stands for everything you despise. Remember that class action suit you defeated for us last year? The claims were all true. The city's been paying the company a special rate to calm and sterilise its problem populations for the past year. Well, I'm through with being my uncle's puppet. I'm leaving, and before I go, I'm going to give the people of Clifton a taste of their own medicine. Something that will make them see that their homes are no safer than anyone else's."

Tony laughed. "Don't be a fool. No one in Clifton drinks the water; they just use it to fill their Jacuzzis and water the lawn. You've picked on the wrong population."

Tony was always like that. Cocksure. Capable of turning white to black, romance to ridicule. Charley wasn't going to let Lucie grow up to be like him. "Then let them be contaminated by their own cappuccinos," she said, pushing past him. "This is one pollutant that won't be defeated by your stupid English tea-drinking habit of boiling the water."

* * *

Back in the office, Hannah was mortified that Syd should know more about a water pollutant than she did. "What is Qartazine?" she asked. "What does it do?"

"Not got it listed in your Bumper Book of Bad Things in the Water?" mocked Syd. "But then you don't get out much, do you?"

"Cut the crap. What are you talking about?"

"QweeZee," said Syd. "Drug of choice round the Bristol club scene ever since our beloved 'Pride and Joy' party got elected. Coincidence? I don't think so."

"Oh," said Hannah, not sure whether to be disappointed or relieved. "So all that'll happen is they'll be getting a free high?"

"You really *don't* get out. It's not a high. It's a power trip. When it hits, you think you understand the whole world. You act like a megalomaniac. You command. You control. And if anyone stands in your way, you kick the shit out of them."

"Who'd want to take that?" asked my mother. It's true she didn't get out much. She didn't have the money for drugs and drinks and clubs; not with the way the interest on her student debts kept going up.

"The proto-Facists who run the council, of course," said Syd. "And their bully boys. They like to distribute it around the clubs. At low doses it makes people very suggestible. Especially if it's mixed with alcohol. It just gives you a lovely, warm sense of belonging to the dominant group. What could be better for an evening out? It even makes it easier to drive when you're drunk."

Hannah finally understood something about Syd. Qartazine, or QweeZee, or whatever it was called, must account for how he managed to drink and still hold down a job. "You take it, don't you?"

"Yes," he said, after a moment of hesitation. "I'm an addict, okay." His sarcasm was tinged with a bitterness she hadn't heard before. "But, F.Y.I., I'm not an alcoholic. The booze is just to stop me from killing anyone. It counteracts the effect of the drug. Without it, I'd be beating up those morons in public relations on a daily basis. Which, come to think of it, might not be such a bad idea..."

Hannah felt ashamed and a bit scared. "How could something like that get into the water?"

Syd shrugged. "Several of the components are already used in water treatment. You'd only have to add the active ingredient."

"What's going to happen when people drink the water?" asked Hannah.

"That will depend on the dose."

"The guys at the control room, they said a whole lorry-load went straight into the supplies," said Hannah. "It was pumped through before anyone realised."

"Then, they'll beat each other up," said Syd. "And they'll beat up anyone else in their way."

In the silence that followed a phone began to ring in the office. Hannah looked at the display: it was Tony.

* * *

While Tony was on the phone to Syd, Charley was in the crèche collecting Lucie, and putting security on standby. Tony could hardly snatch Lucie in front of the massed ranks of the Clifton surveillance cameras, but it was best to be safe. She pulled Lucie's woollen hat well down over her little face, then lifted my sister into her arms and walked outside.

Tony was still there. He had his phone out and seemed to be trying to film them. "You could at least let me see her face," he taunted.

Charley pushed past. "What's the point? She's not your daughter."

"She will be. When I get her back," said Tony. He followed Charley down the road. "What is she to you, Charley? Can't you get your uncle to make you a child of your own?"

Charley wondered for a moment if Tony would believe her if she told him the truth. Probably not. He wouldn't want to believe that his daughter was as damaged as she was.

"You should call your uncle," said Tony, falling into step beside her. "There's some bad news on your project— whoever you bribed for this little revenge trip had another idea. Or maybe someone in the council outbid you. They've taken the chemicals to the wrong reservoir, and pumped them straight into the mains. So I suggest you get the office back on-line and sort it out."

Charley hugged Lucie against her, a warm body between her and the onslaught of the wind. "It's too late then. If it went straight into the mains, people will already have drunk it."

Oh God, she thought. Undiluted. Would they all die? No, of course not. *They'd just kill each other.*

"I can stop it," said Tony. "Just give me my daughter, and I'll do whatever it takes."

"There's nothing you can do," said Charley.

Tony was still with her when she reached the barrier. "Goodbye," said Charley, confident that Tony would be stopped and she'd go through. It took a moment to realise that it was her ID card setting off the alarm.

"Will you give me my daughter now?" Tony said. "I can still help you."

Charley clung more tightly to Lucie. An official, some Neighbourhood Watch nobody, was coming towards her. "You don't understand. Evrémonde's not my uncle. I'm one of his products, designed in his lab. He owns me, just as he owns Lucie. Genetically-speaking she may be your daughter, but in reality she's part of me. And we're both property of the company."

Naturally, my father didn't understand any of this. He just thought that Charley was trying to talk him out of taking Lucie.

* * *

My mother, who'd heard the whole conversation via the phone link and seen the footage of Charley and my sister, knew finally and damningly why she'd been stood up.

"It's not what you think," said Syd. "Tony's only trying to get his daughter back."

"Oh don't bother," said Hannah. Pity from the office freak was the last thing she needed. "I've no illusions about Tony. He can do what he likes. I know he's not going to leave his wife for me."

"Tony doesn't have a wife," said Syd. "Not any more. She went back to Russia after their little girl died."

"Of course he has," said Hannah. Why else were she and Tony creeping around, having an affair? She picked up the family photo on Tony's desk. "See, does she look Russian to you? And that child's a boy not a girl."

"*They're* not his family," said Syd. "It's just a picture he found on the Net. He didn't want people to know about his real family."

"That's just screwed up," said Hannah, not sure she believed him.

"He had his reasons. Remember the cryptosporidium outbreak?"

Hannah nodded.

"The little girl who died was his daughter," said Syd.

"No, she wasn't," said Hannah. "She was the daughter of that activist. From the Road Block."

The Road Block had been the culmination of the carbon-neutral Bristol campaign, a week of blockades, protests, and other anti-car action that had, inevitably, got out of hand.

"That was Tony," said Syd. "Leader of the Road Block."

"What, that bearded twat with the Jesus complex and the stupid home-made clothes? You have to be kidding!" Hannah had hated the Road Block. It was the moment when the city divided into two and she'd ended up on the wrong side, torn between the desire to do her best for the planet, and annoyance over the arrogance of these people who were dictating how she should live.

"Well, he did have a bit of a makeover before he started here," said Syd. "It wouldn't do to have your corporate lawyer looking like a twentieth century hippy."

"The Road Block guy *was* a lawyer," remembered Hannah. "That's why everyone was so surprised when he settled out of court."

"Exactly," said Syd.

And Tony carried around a lot of anger, thought Hannah, there was no doubting that. Even if he pretended otherwise.

"Ask him yourself if you don't believe me," said Syd. "Maybe he'll tell you the truth one day. In the meantime, we have a riot to stop."

"What do you mean, 'we'?" said Hannah. "Why do *we* have to stop the riot?"

"Who else is there?" asked Syd. "Tony can get the water cut off, but we're going to have to deal with what's happening on the streets."

"I think you'll find there's an emergency procedure for all this," said Hannah.

"Yes, but it'd be way too slow, even if half the systems weren't down." Syd seemed extraordinarily focussed, even passionate. "If we don't stop this, a lot of people are going to get hurt."

"But what about Evrémonde? I've got to call him back," said Hannah. "He's relying on me." Or using me, she thought.

"Don't sweat. Tony will tell him everything." Syd opened his desk drawer, took out a plastic bag, and shook two pills into his hand. He offered one to Hannah. "You're going to need this."

Hannah shook her head. She never took drugs, not even from her friends. Not even at parties. Certainly not at work.

"Suit yourself," said Syd. "But without it, you're not going to be much use out there on the streets. It's the only way you can help me control them."

My mother hesitated, then realised she didn't care what it might do to her body. After all, it wasn't as if she were going to keep Tony's baby.

* * *

Charley and Lucie were taken into the security office. Charley showed her papers, and her pass, and demanded to be released. She used her uncle's name. She used the name of the man she worked for on the council. She used everything she could think of. All without results.

Then Tony, as insufferable as ever, strolled into the room. "It's all over, Charley. You've been set up. Your uncle's already disowning you; he's authorised me to start proceedings against you for polluting the water. Oh, and he's giving me custody of Lucie."

Charley felt like laughing. "Go ahead. You'll never get Lucie, not if you put me in gaol."

But Tony didn't believe her, and showed security his authorisation to take his daughter.

My sister remembers this moment, just like she remembers everything from that day. She has the perfect recall of a mind moulded by Qwee-Zee. A mind synced to Charley's since the day she was implanted into Charley's womb. So as Lucie felt herself torn away from Charley and given to a stranger, a shockwave flashed through her. Lucie was too young to understand what was happening, but her baby brain felt everything Charley felt, and at that precise moment it was hatred of Tony—my father and hers. Charley hated Tony so deeply and passionately that Lucie began to scream and howl and kick. Lucie managed to squirm out of Tony's arms and onto the ground, where she lay bawling until Charley was allowed to pick her up again.

* * *

"This is where Syd and Hannah zoom off to save the city," I told the little group. "Only, since neither of them has a permit to drive into Central Bristol, they have to catch the bus."

"What about the Tramzit line?" asked the boy who'd spoken earlier.

"It hadn't been built then," said the researcher. "And they hadn't re-routed the river back through Broadmead either."

The woman was so proud of her second-hand knowledge of Bristol. It was as if the new nation's identity depended on their Bristol past, even though relocation to Somerset, and the process of Assimilation (as the planning reports liked to call it) had changed these people out of all recognition. It was Bristol's final trick against this vibrant Afro-Caribbean community that the authorities had been trying to sideline ever since they first settled in the damaged inner city streets of St Paul's.

"You're right," I told the researcher. "In my mother's day, there was no river there, just a big area of grey concrete underpasses, smelling of piss, at the heart of the city. And that was where Syd went to mobilise his army."

* * *

My mother wasn't surprised that Syd knew all these street people. He *was* the office alcoholic. But she hadn't realised that it was such a big network and that these wild-eyed lunatics were actually human beings, who grasped the situation immediately.

"There's already trouble in St Paul's," said one toothless derelict.

"I heard they were going to smash up The Colston Hall," added a woman wearing five layers of clothes.

"No way! They're too busy fighting," said a crusty with wild grey hair.

Hannah could hear the sirens and felt the city was taking on a life of its own, an expectant hum of violence. At the same time her own senses were extending under the drug's influence, reaching out, inhabiting, and even propelling the people around her, channelling strength and direction from Syd.

"There's only one antidote to this," said Syd. "Alcohol. We've got to give them something to drink."

My mother felt her sense of her own self receding. She began to see the world as if she were Syd. No, not Syd, but a personality inside Syd, the Dickensian street boy he'd once been, the fatherless boy who had put his trust in cider and dogs.

Syd marched his army of tramps and beggars up from the subway, out into streets where the twenty-first century had added yet another layer of grime and decadence to shops and pubs that had been attracting decay ever since they were built. As the troop went along the street, they gathered new recruits, more of Syd's crusty friends and some eco-activists in their homespun natural fibre clothes and low-maintenance haircuts. The activists, who'd been sent by my father, were all carrying armfuls of booze.

As the band of mismatched warriors turned into City Road, Hannah felt herself ready to fight. She'd only ever been in St Paul's at carnival time when it was alive with reggae music, dreadlocks, whistles, and colourful costumes, and the smell of goat curry permeating the streets. Now the streets were empty and dead, haunted by a rank fear, people peering out the windows as Hannah and her new allies walked by.

A van crawled along the road, its loudspeakers blaring warnings against drinking the water. Smashed windows in shops and houses testified that the warning was too late already.

Syd's troops tracked the mob by the noise and came upon them a few streets later. There they were, men and women, black and white, policemen and Rastafarians, old ladies and children, dancing and screaming and laughing and fighting and smashing the rusting useless cars. Hannah and Syd and their band of supporters dived in amongst them, joining in the dance, holding out bottles of cider and beer and cheap wine. My mother, who knew that without Syd's drug and his directing influence she would have been scared and bewildered, joined in the *danse macabre*, sharing her bottle with the jostling, angry mobsters. And so they all danced and drank and pushed and punched until, exhausted one by one, the rioters came back to their senses and crawled away or just lay there on the street.

"Onwards! We have to go on!" shouted Syd. And my mother knew, without his saying, where he was leading the remains of their troops. Syd was taking them to the bridge, where once he had lived—the bridge over the motorway separating one half of the city from the other.

Hannah felt the force of the wind behind her, and a tireless exhilaration in her limbs that she had never known before. And so she and the others ran and tumbled and hurled themselves up against the next mob. The tattered army was running low on alcohol; all the off-licenses were barred shut, but Syd's friends who knew every source of drink in the city talked their way into a pub, and blagged a few bottles of gin and whisky from an old black publican. And so, booze supply replenished, Syd's forces danced and fought their way through to the bridge.

The police sirens were growing louder again. Hannah looked down from the bridge and saw that the motorway beneath her had been shut off and there was a running battle between police and rioters. But there was no time to see the outcome as they were in the thick of the action on the bridge. Syd's gang forced their way forward, but could do nothing but push and elbow, with little chance of sharing drinks in the confined spaces of the bridge. My mother got shoved aside, and fell back onto the tarmac, where she sat, offering Jack Daniels to anyone who came near her. But Syd was still in the lead when a couple of kids with flick-knives charged the crusty army. Hannah saw a knife go in and saw the smile on Syd's face as he went down. And heard the words: "It's a far, far better thing that I do, than I have ever done," (or maybe she made that up later to improve the story) as Syd died on the bridge he loved, too late to see Tony arrive accompanied by a squad of policemen in riot gear.

* * *

And so the battle of the bridge was won, at the place of the bridge. The police made short work of the remaining rioters, and none of them crossed through to wreak further havoc in St Paul's.

Hannah tried to work out what was happening to her. The drug had affected her brain or maybe Syd's brain, in a way that had allowed them to think as one person, and now a part of Syd would forever be in her head. And therefore—let's not forget—forever in mine.

My father sat next to my mother while ambulances came and went, although it was too late for the crews to help Syd.

"Drink?" Hannah offered. The effects of the drug were beginning to wear off and now the world looked grim and dark without the manic happiness that had lit up the margins of the bridge and made it momentarily home for her too. All that was left was a spark, deep down within her, which she could feel growing stronger all the time. The spark of life that was to become me.

Tony took the bottle and tipped it back, just like one of Syd's friends. "To Syd!" he said. His face looked empty and raw without the usual play of expressions that made it alive.

"Did you get your daughter back then?" Hannah asked.

Tony shook his head. "She's not my daughter. My daughter died two years ago."

"Syd told me," she said. "In that cryptosporidium outbreak. I was a junior analyst at the time. I testified at the inquest."

"Yeah, I know. I thought you were a company stooge until I noticed how gullible and bloody conscientious you are."

"Thanks!" said Hannah.

"That incident was the water company's first commission from the new City Council," said Tony. "They wanted me off the streets."

"Because of the Road Block?" Hannah guessed.

"Yes, but I was too bloody busy organising to go back home, even when my wife and child got sick." He paused, seeming to struggle for words. "My daughter died. And I was out stopping traffic."

"Yet you still came to work for the company?" said Hannah.

"Evrémonde promised to clone her," said Tony. "And I thought I could get it all back. Lucie. My wife. My whole campaigning, self-righteous life. But she's not Lucie. It's just a little girl who looks like her."

Down on the motorway, police sirens were still sounding, and my mother could see flashes of blue light reflecting on the parapet of the bridge like light from an unsteady, alien sun. "Didn't you ever consider there might be an easier way?" she asked.

Tony shook his head. 'There is no easy way. I don't want any other child."

"I'll call him Syd," said my mother, making sure he understood. "And tell him what your friend Syd did to save the city."

Tony laughed. "Syd did exactly what they wanted. Saved St Paul's and gave the council the excuse they need to tighten up security. They've been squeezing out the black population for some time, buying up their houses and resettling them in Bridgwater. If the Bristol First Party wins again at the next local elections, the area will be all white by the end of the decade. And with a hero like Syd to use, how can they fail?"

* * *

"So that's how it was that Syd, the alcoholic and drug addict, became a local hero in Bristol, and St Paul's was saved for posterity but lost to its own people," I told my audience. "The footbridge over the motorway was pulled down and a monument built next to the Barriers that had kept North Bristol safe from the lawless areas on the other side of the motorway."

"What about Tony and Hannah, did they ever get married?" asked the researcher. I don't think she cared, but she wanted it all on record.

"No, though they did live together for several years."

"And Charley?"

"She was bailed out from prison by her uncle but was killed in a freak accident while travelling through the Channel Tunnel. Everyone thought my sister Lucie had died at the same time, until my father turned up with her one day. I don't know whether Tony ever forgave her for not being his Lucie, but as she grew older she sounded more and more like Charley Evrémonde."

The researcher seemed satisfied. The leader of the delegation thanked me and went to check that the City of Bristol authorised recording had captured it all.

"How come more people didn't use this Qartazine stuff to pass on their memories?" the dark, muscular guy asked, as the remaining delegates prepared to leave. "We could do with something like that for our fractal."

"There were lots of court cases about it. My sister claimed they'd violated our human rights. So eventually it was banned."

"Shame." I could see the ambition in his eye. An echo of that lust for power, which Hannah had seen in Valèry Evrémonde. "I bet you can get it somewhere. Evrémonde's still alive, isn't he? He must be using something."

"He's been frozen," I said. "My sister's in charge now."

Or at least, that's what I hope.

But for me, the reality of my life is not about power or competing personalities. Hannah's story is my story because I remember everything that happened to her as if it happened to me. The link built between us by the drug when I was developing inside my mother never broke. All my life I've had her memories, and she's felt what I felt. Up until the day she died. Leaving the question unanswered: am I her, or is she me?

Now that I'm old, I remember Hannah's life better than my own. Or maybe I just prefer her past, and the wild and dangerous Bristol that she used to live in. That age of contradictions and greed that no one really understands anymore. No one wants it back, but still they come and listen to me, and deep inside their altered minds I can tell that there is something that still yearns for the passions and purposefulness of those days.

Trespassers

By Nick Walters

Crouching uncomfortably in the bushes at the edge of the Avon Gorge, Simon wished—not for the first time—that they'd gone to the pub instead.

Matt was fiddling with his camera.

"What are you doing?"

"Just putting in some fresh," Matt whispered back.

Simon glanced around. Everything was quiet, which was just as it should be; it was gone two o'clock on a Wednesday morning. To his left, shining through the leaves and branches above him, the lights of the Clifton Suspension Bridge picked out the structure of the famous landmark in bright orange blobs. It looked close enough to touch. In front of him, the main road—Sion Hill—led up towards Clifton Down and in the other direction past the Avon Gorge Hotel and down into Clifton itself.

"Ready," said Matt, tossing the dead batteries into the bushes. Simon frowned. Sometimes his friend seemed to have no respect for the environment, for history, or anything much.

The sound of a car engine alerted Simon to danger; he retreated further into the undergrowth, and listened in apprehension as a vehicle—out of sight from their hiding place—braked outside the hotel. A sudden burst of voices, a girl's shrill laugh, horribly loud in the stillness.

"What the hell are people doing out this late?" muttered Matt, thrusting the camera back in its pouch.

"We'd better hang on a bit longer," said Simon.

Matt snorted.

Simon ignored him as the vehicle—a taxi—emerged into view and coasted off up Sion Hill, its orange light flicking on as it passed them. In a few seconds it was gone.

Simon looked up at the bulk of the hotel. It was practically breathing down their necks. "That's our problem," he said. "Cities never sleep, and people go in and out of hotels at all hours."

"Nonsense, we'll be out of cover and in within seconds. If you follow my instructions." He reached into his rucksack. "Here."

Simon found something warm and woollen thrust into his hands.

"Put it on," urged Matt.

It was a balaclava.

"I'm beginning to think that this is a really, really bad idea," said Simon as he slid the thing over his head. It smelled like someone's old hiking sock. "You could at least have washed the thing," he groaned.

Matt had also donned his balaclava, and it struck Simon that they must look like SAS hard-nuts. Or terrorists.

Matt slung his rucksack over his shoulders. "Right, ready?"

Simon's mouth was dry. "I don't think I'll ever be ready."

Matt glanced briefly to the heavens and fixed his friend with a steady glare. "Look, this is small stuff. People have already been in here—there's a Clifton Rocks Railway Restoration Society, even *open days*, for fuck's sake! This is safe, not really a proper urban exploration at all."

"Yeah, you're the seasoned explorer; I'm just a newbie. Keep rubbing it in, why not?"

"Look, mate, we could have done somewhere really risky, like the old Courage Brewery. Seen the security there? Or the ParcelForce sorting office. Kids have died mucking about in there!"

Simon didn't need reminding about the dangers of urbex, but Matt was on a roll.

"I've done it all. I've been in more abandoned mental hospitals than you probably even know exist. I've been down storm drains, almost got drowned once. And I was in a tower block in Perivale an hour—*one hour*—before they blew it up!"

"I know; I've seen your blog." It had been Matt's blog that had got Simon into urbex. It intrigued him that cities, the most densely-populated areas on the planet, could harbour these forgotten, neglected sites. That he could be living unknowingly bang on top of somewhere dark, empty, unexplored, forbidden. A neglected record of the past, papered over by progress.

"Then you'll know," said Matt, "that you're partnering a serious, seasoned practitioner."

Simon had known Matt since uni, but urbex was something Matt had got into since then. "Look, I know this seems safe to you, but I doubt you were as cocky your first time. And however you dress it up, we're still breaking in!"

Matt grinned. "That is what makes this a proper urbex! Now—come on!"

Keeping low, they dashed across the lane. In the wedge this made with Sion Hill was the Top Station of the Clifton Rocks Railway, a subterranean structure bordered by stout pillars, forbidding Victorian cast-iron spiked railings, and a locked main gate along the Sion Hill side. They made for the gate; although it was, like the railings, topped with gold-painted spikes, it was slightly lower, and therefore easier to climb over.

At least, that was the theory.

Matt slipped off his rucksack and tossed it to Simon, who caught it by the straps. He then shrugged off his thick jacket and laid it across the top of the railings. Then in a flash he was up and over and beckoning to Simon to follow. His mind a blur, Simon passed both rucksacks over the railings and then heaved himself over the cushioned gates, which rattled alarmingly. Despite the protection of the jacket, it still hurt, and Simon gasped as something dug into his ribs.

And then with a scramble—and help from Matt—he was in. He glanced wildly around, but there was no one in sight, nothing on the road. Dead quiet.

"That was the easy bit," said Matt, shouldering his rucksack.

They were standing at the top of a wooden-banistered stone staircase, which zig-zagged steeply back upon itself, leading to the hidden platform below. Simon caught a sudden chill, damp waft of air. On the wall to his right was a big red sign—starkly visible in the orange beams of the streetlights—proclaiming that this area was under constant surveillance by Solon Security Solutions.

And up on a nearby lamp-post, the unobtrusive yet unmistakable shape of a CCTV camera.

Matt saw where he was looking and tutted. "We've been over this. All they'll see—that is, if they ever bother looking at the tapes for tonight, which I highly doubt—is a couple of blokes in balaclavas. Nothing to identify us at all. No one will ever know we've been here. And even if they did somehow find out, so what? We're not hurting anyone, we're not vandals."

"The urbex manifesto," teased Simon.

"If you like. Come on!" Matt started down the steps, and Simon followed. He was surprised to see clumps of forget-me-not growing from cracks in the brick walls, like surreal plant-beards, their usually cheery blue and yellow flowers looking like dead eyes in the night.

The staircase took them through a white-tiled archway and back under itself. Ahead, a barred, locked metal gate—and darkness beyond. At least now they were out of sight.

Matt set to work immediately with his set of skeleton keys. Simon looked away, trying not to worry about what would happen if they got caught. If the keys didn't work they really would be breaking and entering.

There was a jangle and a hiss of triumph from Matt, and they were in.

Simon followed him into the darkness, fumbling for his torch, waiting for the signal from Matt. They had to be sure they were completely out of sight before they made any light of their own. The cool smell of damp masonry slid down his throat. He started to feel disoriented, reached out to touch flaking walls, and bumped into Matt.

His friend flicked his torch on, and Simon did the same.

"Jesus," breathed Matt.

They were in an old ticket office, complete with booths and an ancient wooden turnstile. Posters proclaiming the work of the Clifton Rocks Railway Restoration Society festooned the whitewashed walls, as did another helpful reminder from Solon Security Systems.

Doors at the far end led to the long-disused tunnel of the funicular itself.

"Right, the idea is, we go down to the Lower Station, poke around the old BBC studios, see if we can get out onto the Portway, and if we can't, come back up."

Simon nodded, feeling somewhat overwhelmed, a tingle of excitement running along the soles of his feet. He was beginning to see what Matt got out of urbex, how it was possible to get addicted to it. A sudden flash of light made him jump—but it was only Matt's camera. He made Simon take a photo of him with his thumbs up in front of the ticket office. Simon again pondered Matt's lack of respect, but then reconsidered; he and other serious urban explorers really weren't doing any harm, except perhaps to themselves if things went wrong, or they were caught. They never vandalised or stole, but simply observed, documented, photographed, shared. True, they were trespassing; breaking the—or rather a—law; but who did they actually hurt?

Matt strode over to the door to the left of the tunnel and thrust it open. Simon joined him, and they shone their torches down a narrow, brick-walled passage. Concrete steps led steeply down into darkness, bracketed by a metal railing on the left side and a wooden one on the right. Every dozen steps a landing was bordered by tubular metal barriers.

A smell of damp and dust wafted gently over them.

Matt nudged Simon in the ribs. "Good job they put these staircases in during the War. The gradient's pretty steep."

"I know," said Simon tersely. "I am a Bristolian, I do know my history."

"Orl roight moi luvver!" teased Matt, his voice echoing down the passage.

Simon ignored him. He was no local history expert, but he'd checked on the Net. The tunnel of the Clifton Rocks funicular ran at a narrow angle to the platform, and led at a steep gradient for almost five hundred feet down to the Lower Station on the Portway, two hundred feet below through the limestone rock. The stairway before them had been erected after the funicular fell out of use; there was another, similar one on the other side. Between them, the tunnel, where the rails once ran, lay derelict.

Simon noticed that there were bare electric bulbs mounted on the walls near to the crumbling plaster ceiling. A cable linked them and ran to a rudimentary switch near the door. Impulsively, Simon flicked the switch.

Nothing happened.

Matt shrugged. "Probably runs off a generator."

Simon gazed apprehensively into the murk. "Can't we find it and turn it on?"

Matt shook his head. 'Nah. One, we'd waste time; two, it might not have any fuel; three, someone might hear it if it worked. Trust me, it's not worth it." He waved his torch at Simon, briefly dazzling him. "Anyway, we've got these. What are you scared of?"

"Nothing," said Simon.

"Well, go on then," said Matt, gesturing towards the stairwell. "Ladies first!"

Simon curtsied, flicked the V's at Matt, then stepped into the passage.

There wasn't much to see. Every now and then there was a door-sized gap in the brick wall to their right, through which they could see into the main tunnel, but all they found therein were piles of brick, rubble and stone, and the odd twisted, rusted remnant of track.

It was about half-way down, on one of the railed landings, that Simon first heard the noise.

It was coming from somewhere below them, a tapping, scuttling sound, like someone dragging a plastic ruler along the bars of a radiator. It was accompanied by an occasional, alarming, pig-like snort.

Simon turned to Matt. From the look in his eyes through the holes in his balaclava it was obvious he had heard it too.

"What the hell's that?"

"Probably other urbexers," said Matt hesitantly. "Come in at the Lower Station, on their way up."

"Bit of a coincidence they chose the exact same time as us!"

"Yes," whispered Matt. "Right, torches off until we know who we're dealing with."

And he switched his torch off.

Simon fumbled with his, almost dropping it before managing to kill the beam.

In the pitch darkness, the scuttling and snorting sounded even louder and closer.

"That doesn't sound like a person," hissed Simon in Matt's ear.

"Could be an escaped pig," muttered Matt.

At that moment there was a loud, piercing cheeping noise, like the cry of a seabird, only weirdly modulated.

"Fuck!" shouted Simon. He turned and began to stumble blindly back up the steps, crashing into the railing.

Simon felt Matt grab him. "Christ's sake, calm it! Probably someone taking the piss. A few of my mates know where I am, and I wouldn't put it past them." He flicked his torch back on. "I'm going to see what it is."

One of the door-sized gaps was on the next landing below, and it was towards this Matt headed, torch beam steady in his hand. Simon held back, heart hammering, trying to calm himself. Perhaps Matt was right, perhaps it was someone playing a joke, or a bird or animal that had somehow found its way into the tunnel.

He watched as Matt reached the next landing and shone his torch into the main tunnel. He flashed the beam around a bit and then looked up at Simon. "Nothing!" he called.

Matt stepped into the main tunnel, disappearing from view. Simon hastily switched his own torch back on and started down the steps.

Suddenly there was a shout, the sounds of a struggle— that piercing chirping noise again—and the light from Matt's torch went out. From the darkness came a dragging sound, like someone was moving something heavy across rubble. Without giving himself time to think or be scared, Simon ran down the steps towards the gap in the wall and shone his torch through.

He stared dumbly at what he saw. On the sloping tunnel floor, amidst the dust and the rusting rails, was Matt, seemingly unconscious.

And standing over him was a monster.

Simon got the impression of an immense insectile head with compound eyes and powerful pincers, and a great shining segmented body bending over his friend. He watched as the thing reached down with a crab-like claw and gently peeled off Matt's balaclava, tossing it aside like a grape skin.

Simon took a step back, trainers scraping the dusty floor. The thing raised its head to regard him, jaws opening and closing slowly, and Simon broke. He twisted round, lunged for the stairway, but in his haste missed the step and fell. He slid gracelessly down the steps on his rear end. Torchlight threw crazy shadows around him, and his mind was filled with the image of that malevolent insect face.

He came to a breathless halt on the next landing. He shone his torch fearfully back up the stairwell, expecting the thing to appear at any moment. He let a half-laugh, half-sob. Had it really happened? As if in answer, he heard a high-pitched chirrup. Shit—it had. And it had Matt.

He had to go back up. But he couldn't move. Simon gnashed his teeth, let out a choking sob, felt tears come. Why was he such a bloody coward? His head felt hot, his temples throbbed. He tore off the balaclava and tossed it down the stairs. Then he saw the light. It was coming from somewhere below; a faint, watery radiance.

Was there someone else down there?

Another one of those insect things?

Simon got to his feet and felt himself walking slowly down the steps towards the light. He could see that it was coming from another of the gaps in the tunnel wall, a ghostly luminescence that played slowly across the wall opposite in a repeated pattern. Like something being projected.

And he could hear singing.

Singing!

A female voice, singing a wordless, fluting tune, which rose and fell like a lullaby.

Simon felt as though he was floating. None of this was happening. He was lying in bed the morning after a legendary night out, and this was some sort of hyper-real dream. Almost in a trance, he walked down the steps to the gap in the wall and looked through.

He stood there immobile for a while, not knowing what to think or do.

A young woman was crouched on the sloping floor of the tunnel, poking around in the dust with what looked like a silver pen. She was clad entirely in a silvery jumpsuit, which glittered in the light of a tennis ball-sized globe rotating, apparently unsupported, in the air above her head. She had immense plumes of fluorescent pink, yellow, and green hair, which radiated out from her head in bizarre patterns, and the skin—on her hands, on her face—was pale blue. Her song floated around the tunnel, pretty yet somehow careless, as though she'd accidentally discovered the tune.

After a while she sighed, slipped the pen-like device into a pocket on the thigh of her suit, and looked up to see Simon. She gaped in obvious surprise.

Her face was beautiful, yet somehow frighteningly so. She had human features, but they were all exaggerated: her face was heart-shaped, pixie-like; the mouth was wide and full, the nose small and pert, and her eyes were large and slanted—and completely black, as if they were all pupil.

She stood up until she was face to face with Simon. She was about six feet tall, taller than him, and her body, he could tell from the tight-fitting suit, was slim and toned.

She put her hands on her hips and smiled. Her lips were dark blue, her teeth small and many.

A confused flurry of images flickered through Simon's mind: the forget-me-nots, Solon security, Matt's balaclava'd face, the insect thing. He felt himself about to cry again, but forced the tears down. "Who the hell are you?" he blurted out at last.

The strange woman held up a long-fingered hand. "Got it! Old Earth English. Sorrys I not word perfect, but it's a language I has not spoken for over a century."

Her accent was strange—somewhere between Russian and German, but nothing like either.

"What the fuck is going on?" demanded Simon. "What's that"—he gestured towards the darkness back up the tunnel—"monster?"

She flapped her hands dismissively. "Oh dears, don't be afraid. My name is Auroone. I won't harm you; neithers will that 'monster' as you calls him. He's Royal Prince of Scintillus Three! And he be my friend."

Simon nodded dumbly.

* * *

This had to be a hallucination, thought Simon as he followed the strange woman—Auroone—back up the steps to where...

"Your Matt is perfectly safe," said Auroone. "Prince is...vegetarian. And pacifist, like all his race."

Race. As in alien race.

"Right," said Simon dreamily.

Above them the light-globe bobbed, casting its lava-lamp shapes on the brick walls. Simon was glad of it—he'd lost his torch somewhere along the way.

"Your Matt probably scared him," chided Auroone.

Simon remembered the terrifying insect face. "Probably."

They came to the gap in the wall where Simon had left Matt with the thing that Auroone called the Prince.

Auroone stepped through, and the light-globe bobbed obediently after her. Simon followed.

Matt was curled up in the dust, sobbing softly as the giant insect bent over him. When it saw Auroone it straightened up and chirruped a welcome. To Simon's surprise, Auroone chirruped back.

She turned to Simon. "Prince tells me your Matt is in shocks." She touched his arm. "Go to him, reassuring him, help."

Trying to ignore the giant insect, Simon went to Matt and touched his shoulder. "Matt? Mate? It's okay. Look, I dunno what's going on. I think it's a dream; but these...these people seem friendly."

Matt raised his head. His black hair was dusty, and his face was streaked with tears and dirt. Simon had never seen him like this.

"People?" he croaked weakly. He then caught sight of Auroone and sat up abruptly. "What–the–*fuck?!*"

"Hello!" said Auroone.

Matt cackled. "Christ on a fucking bike!"

The giant insect chirruped loudly and Auroone laughed, a harsh trill of sound that echoed down the tunnel.

Matt began to stumble around, waving his arms. "All right, where's the hidden camera? What is this, some new reality TV shit?" He pointed a trembling finger at Auroone. "Where the hell did you get that costume? Are you auditioning for a part in *Doctor Who* or something?"

Simon tried to placate his friend. "Matt, I think they're for real."

"Yeah, right!"

"Yes—right!" trilled Auroone. "My name is Auroone and this is Prince." Here she made a series of clicks and chirrups. "We explorers. I from Vixenis Major and the Prince is from the Hives of Scintillus Three. Where you from?"

"Wait—you're an alien? From outer space?"

Auroone nodded and smiled, revealing those teeth again. "Alien, yes! I'm a Vixenite!"

Matt laughed madly, making Simon worry that he was losing it big-time. "A sexy space vixen and the bastard son of Alien! This has got to be some sort of wind-up!" He pointed at something on Auroone's belt. "You've even got a ray gun!"

Auroone unholstered the "gun" and held it up. It looked like a futuristic hairdryer, shiny and silver with red fins along its barrel. She laughed. "This isn't a gun! It a matter disintegrator. I supposing it could be used as a weapon." She holstered it again and brought out a slim, tubular, two-pronged device. "*This* is my gun. Rarely do I need to use it, but sometimes..." She smiled sweetly.

"Come on," said Matt. He grimaced in anger. "Who set you up to this?"

Simon stepped forwards. "Calm down, Matt. I think they're telling the truth. Look at Prince whatever—how can you fake that? And that smell..."

The Prince did indeed smell, foully, a sickly-sweet chemical odour.

Matt still looked dubious. "Okay, okay, if you're not here to wind us up," said Matt, "what *are* you doing here?"

"We explorers," said Auroone again. "We find abandoned planets, have poke around, sometimes discover things. It our hobby!"

It struck Simon like a thunderbolt. "Matt, they're urbexers! Just like us, only on a much bigger scale! Not urban explorers—*planet* explorers!"

"Hang on a minute," said Matt. "Abandoned *planets?* Earth's not abandoned. We alone should be proof of that."

Auroone shook her head. "Earth been derelict for, ooh, ages. No one here but we—and you."

Simon felt his blood run cold. "What do you mean 'derelict'? What happened?"

Auroone shrugged. "Dunno. Some sort of war? Or was it a plague. Or meteor?"

The Prince chirruped.

"Supernova!" Auroone said, clapping her hands.

"Holy shit," said Simon.

"Don't worry!" said Auroone cheerfully. "It all right now, radiation has simmered down to safe levels, but Earth still out of bound. That why we here—more fun when it illegal."

"They really are like urbexers," muttered Simon. "But hang on—what you're telling us can't be true. What fucking supernova? It's 2008, for God's sake!"

Auroone frowned, looking serious for the first time since Simon had encountered her. "Big oh. Very big oh. I think I knows what happened." She then chattered to the Prince in what Simon realised must be his own language. Their conversation quickly became heated, with Auroone gesturing with her long, slender arms and the insect's mandibles jiggling busily.

"This could still be a wind-up," said Matt to Simon, who was glad to see his friend had calmed down somewhat, though he was clearly in denial. "Play it cool until we know what's really going on."

Auroone turned back to them, smiling again. "It not 2008, whenever *that* is. It Third Quarter of Sector 93 of Galactic Era Twelve, at least, it is where I come from."

"What the hell does that mean?" cried Matt.

"It means they're from the future," Simon said, feeling a great hollowness expand within him. "They're from the *fucking* future, and Earth is history!"

"Or you from the past," said Auroone.

Images of time tunnels, rifts, and swirling vortices flickered through Simon's mind. "Surely we'd know if we'd travelled in time!"

Auroone waved a hand. "Not. Temporal folds are invisible, intangible."

"No way!" said Simon. "Surely we'd feel something? Or at least hear, see something?"

Auroone shook her head. "Not necessarily. Entropic kick-back occur in higher dimensions, probably 7 or 9—so theory goes. I not expert."

"What the fuck is she talking about?" muttered Matt.

"Shut up!" hissed Simon. "So where you come from, time travel is possible?"

"Not in sense you mean. No control. Temporal folds are natural quirk of nature. No one ever been able to replicate them, thank the suns—time travel would really fark up the universe. There many theories about the folds—I not really understand—but little proof." She grinned widely. "*You* proof!"

The Prince chittered excitedly, and Auroone laughed.

"Wait a minute," said Matt slowly, looking around at the walls of the tunnel, the serene patterns of the light-globe. "If there's no way of telling if we've gone through one of these temporal folds, then it could be you two jokers who have come *back* in time, to 2008."

Auroone looked startled, just for a brief moment. "Oh noes! That would be...inconvenient." She exchanged more chirps with the Prince, who then began to scuttle up and down the tunnel alarmingly quickly.

"Don't mind him. It his turn to impregnate the Chitinoid Queen this year. He go mad if he miss it."

"So," said Simon, "we're either trapped in the future, or you're trapped in the past. There's only one way to find out. We have to go back outside."

* * *

The strange procession set off back down the stairs, the light-globe bobbing silently above them: Auroone in front, Matt and Simon following, and the Prince bringing up the rear. The giant Chitinoid hadn't stopped chattering since Auroone had broken the news about their possible temporal marooning, and it was beginning to get on Simon's nerves.

Funny how quickly you can get used to things, he thought—even things as terrifying-looking as the Prince.

He examined the tunnel walls for signs that they may indeed be in the future, but it looked exactly the same as it had when they'd first broken in. Or did it? Now he came to look, the brick walls looked dirtier, grimier, almost black in places. And the light bulbs and connecting cable were nowhere to be seen. And the concrete steps were thick with dust. But wasn't it just like that in this section of the tunnel? He tried to remain calm. They couldn't be in the future. Could they? He began to see the appeal of retreating into denial.

Soon they reached the bottom of the stairway. They emerged from a short passage into a low-ceilinged, square-ish room piled with rubble. Daylight shone in from a triangular gap at one corner of the room where walls met ceiling.

Auroone grinned. "That where we came in!"

He could see where something—probably the Prince—had shoved some of the rubble aside.

Matt was scrambling up towards the gap, sending stones and grit skittering down towards them. Auroone laughed as she watched his legs vanish through the hole, then followed after him.

From outside, Simon heard a howl of anguish.

"Shit." He looked at the Prince, and the giant insect stared back at him with its massive, inscrutable compound eyes. "Sounds like it's your lucky day, mate."

The creature chirruped once, almost as if it understood him, and was up the pile of rubble and out the hole in seconds.

I could always go back, thought Simon, hesitating, staring at the white triangle of sky. Go back up the stairs, back to the Top Station. Maybe the time tunnel or whatever was still there, maybe he'd get back to his own time. But he couldn't leave Matt. And, despite the dread which weighed on his heart, he just had to *see.*

He started to climb towards the light.

* * *

The river was hidden, its banks choked with giant, distorted, thorny-looking trees, their trunks black and twisted. Rank, red-veined weeds with grotesque white flowers like pouting mouths grew everywhere. Ahead of where Simon stood, between the Lower Station and the River Avon, should have been a road; the Portway, one of the major routes into Bristol. Now there was nothing to show there had ever been a road, just dusty, dry, cracked earth, the red tendrils of weed snaking across it like the veins of some giant beast.

The air smelled fresh and clean. There was a slow, warm wind moving along the Gorge. No sign of animal or bird life. As far as he knew, they were the only people on the planet.

Simon looked up and to his right, where he should have been able to see the Clifton Suspension Bridge spanning the river. There was nothing there at all now, just the rocky walls of the Avon Gorge, wildly overgrown with vegetation.

Simon found it ironic that Brunel's famous creation should crumble to dust whilst the Clifton Rocks Railway, humbler but no less impressive in engineering terms, had survived, protected from the elements by the limestone rock surrounding it.

On the left, further down the river, there was no sign of the city of Bristol at all.

Over it all shone the same old sun, high in the clear and cloudless sky.

Matt was standing near one of the twisted trees. As Simon watched, he reached out to touch its bark. Hearing Simon approach, Matt turned. His face was blank.

"So we are in the future," said Simon.

Matt nodded dumbly. "Fucking hell," was all he could say.

Auroone sauntered over to them. In the daylight, her silver suit gleamed like mercury, and her wild coloured hair and blue skin looked even more strikingly beautiful and alien. Simon watched as the light-globe, now no longer required, deflated like a balloon and snuck into a pocket on the arm of Auroone's suit.

The Prince regarded them with its inscrutable compound eyes.

Auroone seemed—and probably was—blithely unconcerned about the plight of the two men from what was now the past. She smiled at them and pointed upwards.

Something was descending, fast, out of the grey-white sky. An angular, dark object, getting bigger and bigger, and with it an elephantine scream of a downblast of hot air and dust that blinded them.

Grabbing each other for support, Matt and Simon staggered in an unseeing dance until Simon felt his shoulder bash painfully against the stone wall of the Lower Station.

The ground seemed to shudder as something enormous touched down on the remains of the Portway.

Simon opened his eyes to see a massive object blotting out the sky. Its main body was a bulbous grey-green cylinder busy with fins and protrusions and decals, scarred with black scorch-marks and pitted with tiny impact craters. The whole thing was supported on three enormous rust-coloured struts, its bulbous snout cocked like a gun at the sky.

"My ship," said Auroone. Simon could hear the pride in her voice.

It wasn't what Simon had been expecting—something sleek and silver, or possibly some sort of saucer-shaped UFO. The thing looked like something built to explode, rather than fly.

"It old Vixenite raiding barque. I pimped it up myself. Warp engines from a Valethske battle cruiser!"

Matt stood in the shadow of Auroone's ship, his face pale, fear widening his eyes. "No..." he kept muttering, over and over again.

"Matt, what's your problem?" Simon shouted. He couldn't help himself. "We're in the future! We have a whole new universe to explore! Doesn't that excite you?" Simon thought of his flat, his job, his dull single life. The thought of going back to that made his heart sink. "Nothing—nothing that's happened to us up to now matters!"

"He right!" said Auroone. "You come with us, you be well looked-after!" She laughed. "Never need to worry about anything again. Paradise!"

Matt narrowed his eyes. "What do you mean? What are you going to do with us?"

The Prince loomed at Auroone's side. The two aliens exchanged chirrups.

"We simply explorers, like you. You come with us, explore galaxy!"

"I don't want to come with you," said Matt. "I'm going back."

He turned and headed back to the dark mouth of the entrance to the Lower station.

The Prince moved to intercept him, blocking the entrance.

Auroone's musical voice was harsh. "You can't go back."

"Why not?" demanded Simon.

Auroone shrugged. "Folds never reoccur in same place; they only last a nanosecond anyway. You'd be extremely lucky."

"Well at least let us try!" cried Matt.

"Yes, let him try," said Simon.

"Rights!" Auroone chirped, the Prince stepped aside, and Matt disappeared into the darkness.

Simon hesitated, unsure whether or not to follow him. "Does he have a chance?"

Auroone and the Prince were having one of their hurried conferences in the insect's language. Auroone turned and laughed. "None at all. But no harm to let him find out for himself. We in no hurry."

That final statement struck Simon as odd, but he let it pass.

"Come for a ride?" said Auroone, pointing at the ship.

"What about Matt?"

Auroone waved a hand at the retreating figure. "The Prince will stay behind, pick him up when he realise futility."

So saying, Auroone made for the ship. Simon followed into the shadow of the vessel, his guilt at leaving Matt to the tender mercies of the giant alien insect submerging beneath a mounting sense of excitement. He regarded Auroone's pert buttocks beneath her tight and gleaming silver jumpsuit. Apart from the blue skin, the eyes, and the teeth, she could almost pass for human. And the way she'd been looking at him...he shook his head, laughing to himself. That morning he'd not known anything beyond the daily routine, now here he was lusting after a blue-skinned alien female like Captain Kirk on Viagra.

A hatch opened in the side of the ship, a web-like ladder extruded, and Auroone beckoned for Simon to follow.

He glanced back and saw the Prince vanish into the Lower Station, and hoped that Auroone was wrong, that

Matt was able to get home. As for himself, he was now a citizen of the future.

* * *

The flight-deck of Auroone's ship—the Spacemoth— was a large bowl-shaped area dominated by a hemispherical window. The floor of the bowl was laced with webbing, straps, and hand-holds "to assist movement in zerogee," she explained. In the centre were two flight chairs, a conventional one for Auroone and a fearsome contraption like a dentist's chair designed by a madman for the Prince. The walls were decorated with banks of instruments that looked to Simon more like art than technology, and there was a pungent aroma in the air, like patchouli oil mixed with petrol.

Auroone pulled down an auxiliary seat from the hatch and motioned for Simon to sit.

As he did so he realised they were already in flight. The window—which Simon realised with a sickening lurch—was not a window, but a screen displaying a dizzying array of flight statistics and bizarre symbols in every shade of neon, plus a bewildering selection of views from outside the ship, showing a view of the overgrown river and the dead city beyond. Simon was astonished by the amount of greenery. It was almost as if Bristol had never existed.

"How...how far in the future are we?" he asked as he strapped himself in.

"Hard to tell. 2008 mean nothing to me, and Third Quarter of Sector 93 of Galactic Era Twelve mean nothing to you?"

Simon shook his head. "Must be thousands of years..." He remembered what Auroone had said about a supernova. Couldn't have been the sun, that would have wiped the planet off the slate entirely. He wished he knew something about astronomy. "Do you know what star it was that went supernova?"

Auroone tapped a keyboard on the arm of the chair. "Computer...say Eta Carinae. Happened about ten thousand year ago."

"And Earth is now a forbidden zone?"

Auroone giggled with glee. "Yes! Fun!"

Simon ignored her lack of tact and sank back in his seat. "Okay, so Earth's done for—but what about the human race?"

Auroone turned to look at him. "Scattered."

"Scattered?"

"There no pure-bred humans left. Human race abandon Earth, spread out into stars, augment themselves, interbreed..." There was a gleam in her jet-black eyes that Simon decided to interpret as encouraging.

"So what do we...? What do humans look like now?"

Auroone frowned. "Nothing like you. Bigger. Better designed." She laughed shrilly. "You retro! That pink skin not made for space travel!"

Simon grabbed the arms of his chair as the Spacemoth took a dizzying turn, circling the dead city and following the route of the river. "Were your lot once human then?"

Auroone looked insulted. "No ways! I Vixenite. We friends with humans, well now we are, after unfortunate war. We trade, tech transfer, even have sex—but we can't interbreed. Incompatible DNA."

Again that gleam. But Simon saw something else behind it now but couldn't decide what.

"Okays, time we see if Prince has found your friend."

Simon remembered Matt with a guilty lurch in the pit of his stomach. Once more, he hoped Matt had found the fold and got back home. He wondered what he would tell everyone, or even if he would.

The Spacemoth performed an ear-popping, stomach-churning descent. Images whirled across the screen. Simon caught a glimpse of Matt, seemingly out cold, draped across the back of the Prince—but then it was gone. There was a sudden thud and they were down. The screen flickered and then showed a view of the overgrown river.

Auroone turned to smile at Simon. "Okays, we go out to look for our friends?"

Simon nodded, not wanting to give a hint at what he'd seen.

Auroone unstrapped herself and made for the exit tube. Simon fumbled with his restraints and followed, swallowing hard. His earlier confidence had vanished the moment he'd seen Matt and the Prince. What was going on? Was he dead? He clambered down the web-ladder and dropped to the ground.

The Prince was bending over the prone body of Matt, and Auroone was conversing with the creature in its own language again.

Simon strode up to them and knelt beside his friend. He felt for a pulse—thank God, it was there. He looked up at Auroone, fighting to keep his voice level. "What did it...what did the Prince do to him?"

"Prince tells me he stung your friend when he got hysterical when could not find fold."

Simon glanced at the entrance to the Lower Station. Was she telling the truth? Or had the creature got to Matt before he could even look?

"We need to get him back on ship, he can recover there."

Simon considered grabbing his friend, making a run for the tunnel—but there was no way. Even if the fold existed, he'd never find it carrying Matt, and the aliens would never let him get away. Or would they? They seemed friendly. Did he want to test that?

And then he noticed what Auroone was carrying. A slim, tubular device with two silver prongs. Hadn't she said that was her gun?

He decided he didn't want to find out. "Okay."

To his alarm the Prince picked Matt up and clambered up the side of the ship, to a hatch which had opened on the top of the cylinder.

* * *

Back inside the ship, Auroone took Simon along a cylindrical corridor, which ran back from the flight deck, to a small room aft which she called the "sick bay." It had two beds, was cluttered with bits of equipment, and looked like it hadn't been used for ages.

"I leave you friends alone," said Auroone and stepped out. The door hissed closed behind her.

Matt awoke with a groan.

"You all right?"

"Yeah...what happened? Where am I?"

"Do you want the bad news, or the even worse news?"

Matt groaned. "Shit. The aliens."

"Did you find it? Find the fold?"

Matt sat up, putting his head in his hands. "Went up towards the Top Station, but the way was blocked. Rockfall or something; must have happened years, centuries ago. Went up and down the stairs, looked everywhere, but what was I looking for? Then that thing got me. Again."

Simon sighed. "So we'll never know."

Suddenly an image appeared in the middle of the room—Auroone, only a flickering ghost. A hologram, Simon realised.

"We leaving now. I advise you strap tight into the beds—we jumping out of atmosphere."

"Hang on!" said Simon. "Where are we going?"

"Mardus Three!" chirped the image of Auroone, as if that explained everything.

Simon tried the door. It was locked. "Let us out."

The holo of Auroone shook its head.

"What's going on?" cried Matt.

Auroone smiled. "We not just explorers. We scavengers too!"

That smile. Those teeth.

Those shining black eyes.

"Anything we find, we take. And you *great* find!"

At last Simon understood all those looks she'd been giving him. Avarice. Images filled his mind. The Suspension Bridge. The forget-me-nots. The ticket office. Solon Security. His shitty flat, his shitty job, his annoying workmates, the emo girl in facilities management he fancied. UK Gold, a pint of lager, his mum. Things he would never see again. He felt tears come, angrily wiped them away.

Matt, his face blank, was strapping himself in the bunk. "Better do as she says," he said in a hoarse whisper.

Simon stumbled towards the other bed, and was just in time to strap himself in before the Spacemoth jumped to lightspeed.

"You unique, men from past. Pure-blood humans! You going to Science Zoo on Mardus Three. They look after you well. Very well. For many years..."

The image of Auroone vanished like a light being switched off.

Pirates of the Cumberland Basin

By Joanne Hall

The woman's body splayed against the glass dome of the abandoned shopping centre. Sliced from throat to pubic bone, flaps of skin stretched out on either side of her torso, throwing a silhouette like a gigantic bat against the glass. Looking up, Harry saw where she struck the dome, a spider web of cracked glass, and a long smear of blood as she slid to her final resting place.

"Berkley, can you get closer?"

His partner said nothing, overwhelmed by the grim spectacle of the Circus. He lowered the paddle into the murky water, propelling them forward. The only sounds were the soft splashing as the dinghy inched through the Circus, and a persistent dripping from all around, echoing in the stillness.

Harry fixed his eyes on the dead woman, preferring that macabre sight to the half-submerged, abandoned shops around him. As Berkley swung the torch, he could still make out some of their names, faded and water-ruined. He tried not to imagine what they might have sold. That was a world long gone.

The dinghy struck something underwater and came to an abrupt halt, the stern swinging round sharply. The woman's body loomed twenty feet above, pale and distorted in the wavering torchlight. "Now what, Harry?"

Harry wasn't sure. He had to take a sample so InfoCon could find out who she was, tell her family. If she had a family, if she wasn't an illegal, travelled thousands of miles for a better life only to end up as a gory window display.

He was surprised the fragile dome had survived this long. If he was careless he could bring the whole roof crashing down, and Ub-hot would have two extra bodies to deal with. But as Berkley swung the torch, Harry noticed a missing pane, barely five feet from the corpse.

His eye-pod vibrated, a fluttering under his lashes like a tic. Victoria's image appeared, hovering just beyond the end of his nose. Even at two inches high, she radiated irritation. "What are you two *doing* in there? You've been ages!"

"Just getting the sample," he assured her. "We'll be back in ten minutes. Any trouble?"

"Not yet, but the locals are getting very interested in the cruiser."

"Back off for a while. I'll buzz you when we're finished." He broke the connection, and the image dissolved.

"Is Victoria all right?" Berkley asked. It was bad manners to Podshare without permission, but even though Berkley would have turned up his music to drown out her voice, he had still seen her hologram.

"Nothing major." Harry took the drone, a sleek black sphere the size of an apple, from his backpack. Using his controller, he steered it towards the missing pane, careful not to brush against anything. It was delicate work, and he hoped Victoria wouldn't buzz back until the operation was complete. The drone vanished behind the filthy glass, but the proximity warning on the controller beeped loudly as it touched the corpse. He manipulated the buttons, and a series of bleeps told him the sample had been collected. Relaxing, he ordered the drone to return, following the same path.

"Are we done?" Berkley asked, as Harry caught the drone and returned it to his pack. "Let's go; this place is weird. What is a Circus, anyway?"

"Somewhere people shopped, I guess." Harry tried to imagine the aisles of the Circus thronging with life, but it was impossible. There was only the cold, the musty reek of mould, and the endless water.

Berkley paddled quicker as he headed towards the entrance. Harry didn't blame him; the oppressive atmosphere was getting to him, too. Pushing through the ivy that trailed over the entrance, he caught a welcome glimpse of blue sky and quickly buzzed Victoria to pick them up.

Berkley stowed the paddle, sighing in relief. "Being in there makes you appreciate how good it is out here, doesn't it?"

Taking in a deep breath, Harry agreed. The calm water threw back reflections of sky and clouds, disturbed only by the occasional gull. They floated above what was once the main entrance to the Circus. On either side, the tops of sunken buildings emerged from the water like bizarre geometric islands. Brightly coloured lines of washing flapped bravely from the roofs, and every zealously-tended window box was a riot of blooms. The city rooftops were a garden, lovingly tended by these upper floor dwellers who had stayed behind when the water rushed in. Their gardens were bright, their clothes garish, but their faces were dour as the little yellow dinghy bobbed past. Conversations hushed, and every eye turned to watch with quiet, futile resentment.

"Where the hell is Victoria?" Berkley muttered, tightening his grip on the oar.

"She'll be here." Harry kept his gaze locked straight ahead. Making eye contact with the roof dwellers invited trouble.

He heard the low throb of the police launch before he saw it. The rooftops emptied, as the long, low cruiser emerged from behind the old House of Fraser building and skimmed up the Haymarket towards them.

Safely aboard, Harry strapped himself into the passenger seat. Victoria smiled. "Did you get what you wanted?"

"A sample. I had to leave the body to the gulls."

"Where to now, then?"

"Ub-hot. Let's see if we can find out who the poor bitch was and how she ended up there."

The scientific division of the city police department occupied the old museum building, all marbled floors and Roman columns. Now it was a labyrinth of flimsy bamboo partitions and signs in three different languages. Harry turned up the music in his Pod to drown out the high-pitched electrical whine that filled the air, but he couldn't evade the hum of the generator, pulsing behind everything like a massive heartbeat. He could feel it in his own chest. It made him nauseous, and he increased his stride, hoping InfoCon would identify the dead woman quickly so he could get out of here.

His metal-tipped heels clicked on the sweeping staircase. On the first floor the greasy, fried-potato smell of the generator was much stronger, making him feel simultaneously sickened and hungry. Opening the double doors, he found himself eyeball to chest with the stuffed gorilla. It was sporting an old-fashioned fedora, the kind archaeologists used to wear. He gave it a nod, and the gorilla nodded back, with the slow wheeze of dying animatronics. Its eyes, replaced by security cameras, followed him as he crossed to Magda's cubicle.

Magda's cubicle was a bright monument to her drowned homeland. It was painted lurid orange, and little Dutch flags jostled for space with the stuffed ducks on her desk. It was like stepping into the heart of a tangerine, and it made Harry's eyes water. Magda was a striking woman, pale, with hair so blonde it was almost white, but her orange mini-dress leached away what little colouring she had, making her look like a ghost. She sat hunched over her machine, swearing at it in Dutch, and only looked up when Harry cleared his throat.

"Hey Harry! What's up?"

He held up the drone. "Sample for you."

"Your mystery body from this morning? Pass it here." She inserted the drone into a slot in the machine. "It'll take a moment."

"I don't mind waiting." He liked hanging around Magda, despite the relentless orange. Her cubicle was interesting, with its fading pictures of long-dead Dutch footballers and pop stars. There was always something new to see. This time it was a newspaper cutting heralding the 2018 World Cup winning Dutch football team. Their smiles were as faded as their strips. "Where do you get all this stuff?" he asked her.

Magda shrugged. "Around." On the black market, of course. Dealing in items from the Drowned Countries was lucrative. People like Magda would pay a premium for memories from their lost home.

She changed the subject. "You're looking peaky, Harry. Are you eating your two portions of meat?"

He snorted. "I don't care what the government says, who can afford two helpings of meat a week?"

She leant forward conspiratorially. "I've got some seal, if you want to barter."

The thought of seal, combined with the smell of the generator, made Harry's stomach gurgle. "Where did you get seal? No, don't tell me, 'around,' right?"

"Right!" She winked. "I'll bring you a portion tomorrow." Her computer bleeped. "Your sample's done. Let's find out who your mystery woman is."

She shifted her chair sideways so Harry could get a proper look at the screen, though the symbols and Dutch text meant nothing to him.

"Her name was Cornubia Penhallow."

"That's quite a mouthful."

"Don't worry, I'll give you a printout." She caught his expression. "And it'll be in English, if you insist. I don't know why you Brits can't learn other languages."

Harry resisted pointing out that Madga, despite her Dutch heritage, was born in Bristol long after the Netherlands were swallowed by the sea, and was as British as he was. Why trample on her romance?

Madga peered more closely at the screen. "That's interesting," she said. "She was registered as living on the *Great Britain*. Her sample tells me she'd recently had a baby—hormones in the blood—but there's no baby registered here."

"Maybe it died."

Magda shook her head, tight-lipped. "It would have been registered anyway," she insisted. "There's a note on her record that she was pregnant, so she must have seen a doctor." She looked up, lines furrowing between her almost-invisible eyebrows. "We can't have unregistered children running about. You'd better find out what happened to that baby, Harry."

"Will do!" He mock-saluted her as he grabbed the paper chuntering out of the printer. "Do you know when she died?"

"I'm not a detective, Harry. I'd worry more about the baby. I guess you should start by looking on the *Britain*. They might tell you something."

* * *

The cruiser bobbed at the edge of the water, halfway down Park Street. Victoria and Berkley were Podsharing in the front seat when Harry returned. He hadn't realised they were so close. Neither of them had ever offered to Podshare with him, and he felt a twinge of envy. He banged on the tempered blue glass hull of the cruiser with more violence than usual. "Enough of that. Time for work."

Victoria broke the connection reluctantly. "Did InfoCon find anything?"

"Yes, and you're not going to like it. Berkley, go to Bemmie Down and break it to Mr and Mrs Penhallow that their daughter is Bristol's latest piece of public art. Victoria, we need to find the *Great Britain*."

Berkley headed back up the hill towards Ub-hot, looking for transport. Victoria glared at Harry, making no attempt to move.

"Victoria?"

"The *Britain*? Are you serious?"

"I don't like it either, but we're looking for an unregistered baby now, as well as a murderer."

She scowled as she twisted her ponytail back into its usual neat bun, pinning it fiercely. "How did that happen? The system's supposed to be perfect."

Harry slipped into the passenger seat. "Something got cocked up. At least, I hope it did."

"And if it didn't? If it's deliberate evasion, rather than a system glitch?"

He left her questions hanging. Maybe the pirates of the Cumberland Basin could provide some answers.

* * *

The *SS Great Britain* was moored in one of her usual spots, tethered to the roof of a building that once housed luxury apartments. Victoria ran the engine down to its lowest speed and let the cruiser chug along. "Should I hail them?"

Harry scanned the ship from bowsprit to stern. At first he saw no signs of life, but as he stared he noticed slight movements in the rigging near the masts. Behind the gunwale, sunlight flashed on metal.

"I think they've already seen us," he said. "Hail anyway, and for God's sake be polite!"

Victoria hailed the dark ship, lying like a shark in the grey water. A heavily-built figure emerged on deck. He had a flag in each hand, waving them in a complicated pattern. Harry and Victoria exchanged glances.

"Is that a signal?" Victoria asked.

"Semaphore," Harry told her. "An ancient form of ship-to-ship communication, according to Infocon. The pirates started using it a few years ago, for some reason."

"Why don't they just use their Pods?"

Harry shrugged, concentrating on the message spelled out by the flag waver.

"They welcome me aboard, alone, and request I leave behind any weapons. And they want me to switch off my Pod."

"I'm sure they weren't so polite," Victoria snorted.

"Take me up to the ship," Harry ordered, fiddling behind his ear. He hadn't switched his Pod off in so long that he had forgotten exactly where the button was.

Victoria looked at him in horror. "What are you doing? You're not going to actually switch it off?"

"Watch the water!" He grabbed the wheel and swung it around. With a shriek of glass on metal, the cruiser scraped along the side of the ship, suddenly looming right above them. "What do you think they'll do, if you've damaged their boat?"

"Bugger their boat. Why did you turn your Pod off? They won't know if you leave it on."

"They might. I'm not going to risk being carved up for it. I can manage without it for a while." Harry felt a lurch in his gut. For all his confident words, he wasn't sure he could.

"So how can I get hold of you?" Victoria's voice was strangely high, and she clutched the steering wheel tightly with both hands.

"You can't. You'll just have to wait for me." With a soft swish, a rope ladder unfurled from the gunwale, and Harry grasped the bottom rung. "If I'm not back in two hours, call Ub-hot."

Victoria nodded, her pale face receding beneath him as he climbed, hand over hand, towards the deck far above. Halfway up, breathless and perspiring, he stopped for a rest. *I'm not as fit as I was in my twenties,* he thought. Hanging there, reluctant to look at the drop below, or the strenuous climb still to come, the ladder swayed slightly in the breeze. Harry was uncomfortably aware of the silence, the isolation. He heard the mewling of gulls, the slop and gurgle of the water, the throb of engines. But the music, constantly playing in his ear, so softly it was like the rhythms of his own body, that was gone, along with the sporadic upgrade beeps of his Pod. He felt small and very alone, brushing gently against the hull of the old ship. If he shouted to Victoria, would she hear him? He opened his mouth, then thought better of it. It felt offensive to break the natural quiet.

"Oi!" The man leaning precariously over the gunwale waving to him clearly didn't share Harry's feelings about natural quiet. "Are you going to hang there all day, copper, or are you coming up?" A large, curved knife flashed in his hand. "I can choose for you, if you like."

"No, I'm coming!" The sweat turned chilly on Harry's back, and he prised his reluctant hands from the rail, forcing himself up the last twenty feet. Strong hands gripped him by the armpits and hauled him onto the deck. A mug of cider was pressed into his hand.

"Get this down, you copper!" The knifeman spoke in a thick Bemmie accent. "It'll steady you after the climb." He grinned, though his teeth were almost hidden behind a thick tangle of beard. He wore a stout wooden plug through his right earlobe, a pink bandanna, and a pair of faded denim shorts. His bare chest was thickly haired. He extended a hand. "I'm Wooky Hoyle."

Harry downed the last of the rough cider with a grimace. "Harry Muller. City Police." He shook Wooky's hand, and took his first look around the deck of the *SS Great Britain*. He had not expected notorious pirates to be so friendly, or so domestic. Washing flapped in the rigging, while children chased chickens around the small cannons installed on the deck. Incredibly, a cow lowed in the byre. Harry was impressed. "Quite a community you have here, Mr Hoyle."

"Call me Wooky." The bearded man frowned. Harry noticed a scar, just below his left eye. "It's a good place, and we don't want any trouble from you, Landpol. What we do on the water is under our own rules. It's those bastards on the *Amistad*," he spat loudly over the side, "you should be talking to."

"And if I talk to them, they'll tell me you're the bastards, and they're just law-abiding pirates, right?" Harry laughed, but Wooky did not join in. His eyes narrowed under uneven brows, and he tapped the knife.

"So what *do* you want, copper?"

The children vanished, their place taken by half a dozen shirtless men, each holding a blade or club. Harry tugged at his collar, longing for the comfort of his Pod.

"I've come to talk to you," he said, careful to keep his voice steady, "about the murder of Cornubia Penhallow. I understand she lived here."

Wooky let the blade fall. "Cornie's dead?"

"We found her body this morning." Harry avoided the gruesome detail. Wooky looked like he was about to throw up.

"And the baby?"

"There was no sign of any baby."

Wooky's curse echoed around the deck like a rifle shot. "In that case, you'd better see Captain Cutler. You should tell him about Cornie."

A door on the deck that Harry had assumed was a cupboard opened onto a narrow metal staircase, leading down into the guts of the ship.

"Follow me." Wooky led him down the stairs. The man's back was as hairy as his front. They passed the great engines, cold and still. Looking down, Harry saw the great steel patches repairing the ship's rusty hull and heard the pumps throbbing. "Don't you worry she'll sink?" he asked. "Where do you get the fuel for the pumps?"

Wooky slammed the engine room door behind them. They stood in a narrow hallway. "Where does anyone get anything these days?" he chuckled. "Barter or theft. You've got no authority here, Landpol, so why does it matter?"

"I was curious. I thought you might have solar panels."

"We've got panels on deck, for heating and suchlike. They'd need to be bigger than the old pitch at Ashton Gate to keep the pumps running all the time!" He grinned, but his smile didn't reach his eyes. Harry wondered what he was holding back.

They ascended another flight of stairs to a long corridor, lined with cabins. "The dining room is just along here. That's where I'm taking you."

An idea struck Harry. "Can I use the bathroom first? I'm a bit sweaty after all that climbing."

"If you need to piss, just say so. No need to be delicate." Wooky opened a door at the end of the corridor. "All proper conveniences here!"

"Proper conveniences" consisted of a bucket and an open porthole, but at least he was alone. Harry flicked on his Pod and spoke in a hushed voice. "Victoria? Are you there?"

Her hologram grimaced. "Harry, are you *peeing*?"

"Only to cover my voice. I'm fine, they seem quite friendly. I've got a meeting with their captain to discuss Cornubia's murder."

"Should I wait?"

The stream slackened. Harry gave Victoria a nod and flashed his upturned thumb, shook off the last few drops, and switched his Pod back off. It was easier the second time. He dried his hands on the seat of his trousers as he returned to Wooky. The pirate regarded him with suspicion.

"Everything all right?"

"Fine," Harry reassured him.

"I thought I heard you talking."

"I sing when I pee. Bad habit."

Wooky chuckled. "Glad I don't live with you, then. Here we are, just up these stairs."

Harry had once seen a movie set in a medieval court. The memory rushed back to him as Wooky threw open the double doors and bowed deeply.

"Captain, may I present Harry Muller, of Landpol?"

Harry hesitated in the doorway, unwilling to bow, but not wanting to cause offence. He settled for an inclination of his head.

"The first-class dining room welcomes Harry Muller, and bids him approach the Captain."

Wooky nudged him. "You're okay," he mouthed. "He'll talk to you."

Long tables flanked the sides of the room, and down the centre, between two rows of narrow columns, ran a moth-eaten strip of carpet. It led to another table, where

Captain Cutler sat in a large, heavy chair. It was a commanding position. The Captain could see the whole room, and windows to either side warned him of any approaching ships. It would be impossible to sneak behind him with a blade. The Captain beckoned him closer, and Harry caught a hint of mischief in his eyes.

"Join me at my table, Landpol. Bring cider for this man!"

Harry declined politely. "I shouldn't be drinking, Captain Cutler. I'm here on duty."

"Taking a nip of cider is hardly drinking. Please, call me Adge."

"Adge Cutler? Sounds familiar..."

"He was a Bristol folk hero, before the waters came. All captains of the *Britain* take the name in memory of him, although no one now remembers why he was famous. I'm Adge Cutler the Seventh, but I was born Ayhan Boral."

"That's Turkish, isn't it?"

The big man grinned beneath his luxuriant moustache. "Quite so! My forebears ran a kebab shop, but I'm the captain of a great ship. But you didn't come here to talk about me." He leant forward, his expression grave. Harry noticed he carried an identical scar to Wooky. "Why have you come aboard?"

"Cornubia Penhallow was found dead this morning, on the roof of the Circus. I understand she was one of your crew. I came to tell you and to let you know you can collect the body. I hoped you could help me find out what happened."

Adge slammed both his hands, palms down, on the table, with a ferocity that made Harry jump. "Are you saying I had something to do with it or any of my crew? We loved Cornubia; she was like a sister, a daughter, to us.

138

What those devils on the *Amistad* did to her—" He broke off, tears welling in his great brown eyes.

"What's the problem between you and the *Amistad*?" Harry asked. "Your man Wooky couldn't mention her without spitting. I thought they were pirates, like you."

"They are pirates, true, but nothing like us. The *Amistad* plies her trade up near the Suspension Bridge, and her crew take on work for Mr Yakamoto. Are you aware of him?"

"No." Harry shook his head, noting the name. InfoCon would have a file on the man.

"That doesn't surprise me. He's the kind of man who takes care not to attract official attention."

"Why would he want to avoid official attention? We leave you pirates alone." An insect buzzed somewhere in the room, a sound Harry wouldn't have noticed with his Pod switched on. Now he found it irritating.

"Mr Yakamoto is not a pirate but a businessman and a land-dweller. That puts him under your jurisdiction, I believe."

"What business is he in? The kind he would want to keep secret?"

The buzzing grew louder, and Cutler's heavy eyebrows knit. "Slavery is an ugly trade, my friend," he said, rising. "Especially in this city." He moved across to the window. "What Mr Yakamoto does goes far beyond that. Did you use your Pod on board?"

"No, of course not," Harry lied. "You asked me not to."

Cutler eyed him coldly. "I hope for your sake you're lying. If not, then you are betrayed. By your pretty pilot, perhaps."

"What are you talking about?"

"Why do you think we cut our Pods out?" The big man indicated his scar. "If you transmit, they can hear you anywhere in the city."

The sound of insects was so loud now Harry felt his head pounding in time with it. Cutler gestured towards the window. A helicopter, rotors spinning, sat on the roof of the submerged flats. It was as stridently orange as the inside of Magda's cubicle, and the men leaping from it wore boiler suits of brilliant red. They moved as one, running lightly up the mooring rope and onto the ship.

"Who are they?" Fear knotted Harry's intestines.

"Yakamoto's men. The only thing that would bring them here is you." Pounding at the door and Cutler leant in close, speaking quickly. "Go with them. Offer no resistance. It's your best chance to find out about Cornubia. She was pregnant when she fled to us from the *Amistad*, and near her time when they took her—" He fell silent, and took a prudent step away from Harry as the door burst open. Two men stood there, short bare swords held across their chests. One of them pointed at Harry. "Muller?"

"Would there be any use denying it?" Harry's relaxed countenance disguised the furious working of his brain, as he wondered how he could contact Victoria. His hand twitched towards his ear.

"Keep still," Yakamoto's man ordered coolly. "You're coming with us." They fell into step around him as they made their way back up to the deck. Two of their companions waited by the mooring ropes, and the pirates skulked in the background. Harry spotted Wooky, lurking by the byre, but the hairy man wouldn't meet his eye.

The man who had previously spoken indicated a plank running from the gunwale to the roof. "We wouldn't expect you to cross by the rope," he said, with a slight smile. "Just take it at a run; you won't fall."

Harry looked over the gunwale at the yawning chasm and the black, sucking water below. "If you say so." He put one foot on the plank, trying to not look down or show tension. It was broader than it first appeared and seemed solid. Taking in a deep breath, he walked, swift and springy, across to the roof of the flats and jumped down. The red men ran along the rope beside him and sprang lightly onto the roof. "Bastards," he muttered.

"Excuse me." The leader reached for his ear. Harry instinctively swatted his hand away.

"What are you doing?"

"Switching your Pod off. Mr Yakamoto insisted on that."

"Did you monitor my transmissions to discover I was here?" Harry scowled. "You know that's illegal."

The man laughed as he flicked Harry's switch. "What are you going to do, Mr Muller? Arrest us? Cut your Pod out, like the crew of the *Britain*? Come on. Mr Yakamoto doesn't like to be kept waiting."

As Harry climbed into the helicopter, he wondered how long it would take Yakamoto's man to realise he had just switched his Pod back *on*.

* * *

Harry had never flown before. He thought he would be terrified, but the prospect of meeting the ominous Mr Yakamoto swept the other concerns from his mind. The image of Cornubia, splayed out on the roof of the Circus, would haunt him for a long time, but flying, even in the vibrating helicopter, was a temporary release from his worries, an unexpected treat. He could see the broad plain of water stretched out below him, dotted with boats. Up ahead rose the elegant span of Brunel's famous Clifton Suspension Bridge, now a mere handful of metres above the slow-moving water. He was quite disappointed when the flight ended, in a fenced-off area of the Downs. They had been in the air only two or three minutes, and he could have happily stayed up there for hours.

"Does this land belong to Mr Yakamoto?" Harry asked. Private land was precious, especially on the Downs.

"No questions!" One of the previously silent men glared at him. Harry pushed his luck.

"Your boss must be very rich. How can he afford fuel for a helicopter?"

"I said no questions!" The heavy raised his hand, and the leader caught him by the arm and addressed him sharply in a foreign tongue. The second man gave Harry a foul look, but let the matter drop.

"Follow me, please." The leader directed Harry and his team to a gate in the metal fencing of the compound and through it into a tunnel made of the same substance with a double-locked door at the end. Ushered through, Harry found he stood at the edge of the water, in elegant parkland. On the far side, the edge of the gorge rose in a tangle of woodland, and to his left, scything across the vista like a great blade, was the Suspension Bridge. He had never seen it so close.

Harry followed his captors towards one of the immense twin towers that supported the bridge on either side of the river. There was a small door in the base of the structure, guarded by two more men in red. The guards let them pass without question, through an elegant marbled entrance hall, up to the double doors beyond.

"You might find this disorientating," the leader warned him, as the doors slid open.

The supporting abutment was a giant honeycomb. Brunel had designed it as a great, secret cathedral, with immense sweeping arches to support the structure. It housed a small, underground town. From where they stood on a broad gantry, Harry could see down a dizzying five stories. Every floor was lit up like a carnival.

"It's incredible, isn't it? There's an even bigger town, on the other side of the river," the leader observed chattily as he drew Harry towards the lifts. Harry tried to take in every aspect of the sight, praying his Pod was recording. Hopefully, if he didn't transmit, they wouldn't notice.

The lift whisked Harry and his captors down to the lowest floor, where they left him to the company of a neat little Asian woman. She swept him through a richly-decorated antechamber, into Mr Yakamoto's office at the base of the abutment. The room was even bigger than the dining salon on the *Britain,* decorated in rich shades of red and orange. There were paintings on the walls and framed football shirts. He recognised some of the names from articles Magda had shown him: Cruijff, Bergkamp, Van Basten. Harry took this in with a glance before turning his attention to Mr Yakamoto. He had formed a picture in his mind of a blustering loudmouth, intoxicated with power, but the man coming forward to shake his hand was dwarfed by his own office. Small and trim, he had wisps of grey in his hair and a kindly smile. Harry supposed he could afford to be kind.

"Mr Muller." Yakamoto gestured for him to sit. "I understand you have been inquiring into the tragic death of Cornubia Penhallow. I require you to stop."

Harry leant back in the chair, a study in calm. He picked up a pen from the desk and toyed with it. "Any reason why?"

"Cornubia worked for me. My own men are looking into it. Further investigations by you will only bring pain."

"I'm sure her family will endure any pain to bring her killer to justice." The pen was topped by a figure of a small boy taking a leak. It looked familiar, but Harry couldn't place it.

"I wasn't talking about her family, Mr Muller."

"I hope you're not threatening me, Mr Yakamoto."

"Call it a friendly warning. You've attracted my attention today; I'll be keeping a close watch on you."

Harry waited to see if Yakamoto would mention his Pod, but the Japanese man merely regarded him calmly, as if waiting for his reaction. Harry wasn't going to give him the pleasure.

"Nice place you have here," he said, casually. "Who did the paintings?"

"They're all copies, but good quality. My family fled Japan after the Rice Wars, with nothing but the clothes they were wearing. I suppose my desire for material possessions comes from them. I always feel it's good to be surrounded by beautiful things."

"Indeed it is." One of the paintings caught Harry's eye. He recognised the print from Magda's shrine.

"Do you like art, Mr Muller?"

"I don't know much about it, to be honest." Harry took a long look at the painting, which was of a pensive-looking girl in a blue and yellow headscarf. Not to his taste. "So you can't tell me any more about Cornubia? Why she ran away from the *Amistad*, for example? Or who the father of her baby was?"

"Who knows the minds of women, Mr Muller?"

Damn, he was as slippery as a politician! "Do you know where Cornubia's baby is now, Mr Yakamoto? The crew of the *Great Britain* is very worried about it."

Mr Yakamoto rose with a sorrowful expression. "So am I, Mr Muller. Please tell Captain Cutler I'm doing all I can."

"So you don't know anything?" Harry slyly pocketed the pissing-boy pen. Magda would probably like it.

"The matter will be taken care of, and you will be kept informed. Until then, if you value your health, I suggest you leave the subject alone. My daughter will show you to the lift." Yakamoto shook his hand and steered him towards the door. The interview was clearly over.

The neat girl, Yakamoto's daughter, handed him over to two new red-suited men, who frogmarched him back to the entrance. "Goodbye, Mr Muller." One of them shook his hand, pressing something into his palm, then vanished back into the abutment, slamming the door. Harry made certain he was out of sight of any watching cameras before he read the sweat-dampened note.

Red Gables, on the Downs, it said. *Because slavery is an ugly trade.*

Especially in this city. That was what Cutler said. Harry wondered why Bristol should be singled out. Slavery was ugly everywhere, surely?

He longed to talk to Magda, but he was sure any transmissions he made would be picked up at once by Yakamoto's monitors. She would know all about the painting and the tasteless pen. He was torn between returning to Ub-hot, on foot and investigating Red Gables. The distance decided him. While he was up here, he might as well check out the house. He could put up with going

145

through Tent Town, but he would have felt much more comfortable if he could transmit.

Tent Town stretched for over a mile across the Downs, a city under canvas. Harry could smell it long before he reached it, a potent reek of human waste and burning plastic. He walked quickly, heels ringing on the metal walkways, trying not to inhale. On the far side of the massive, stinking campsite, there were houses still in private hands. Large ones, with electric gates and guard dogs. Red Gables, Harry was sure, would be one of these.

He found the name on the gate. The house was invisible behind a high wall, topped with iron spikes and a pair of prominent cameras. There was bound to be less visible security, too. He wouldn't get five feet inside the gate without being ripped apart by dogs. He'd have to send a drone and hope no one spotted it.

It took a few nervous, sweaty minutes to link a drone to his Pod, so he could see what it recorded. He wished Berkley was with him; the boy would have done it in half the time and known he was doing it right. He wouldn't be so paranoid, thinking Yakamoto might detect what he was up to. Harry hoped he had programmed the drone to return to Ub-hot when he gave the command word, but he wasn't completely sure.

His preparations complete, he steered the drone in a high arc over the cameras that crowned the gate. It dropped down the other side, showing him a view of a well-manicured lawn and a wide, three-storey house of grey stone. There was a steel grid across the front door and bars on the downstairs windows, which were closed despite the summer heat. No way in there, so he guided the drone around the side of the house, lifting it high over the head of a Doberman snoring on the path.

As it swung round the back of the house, the drone's sensor picked up the squeals and shrieks of children at play. Harry steered towards the sound, keeping it high, hoping no one would look up.

There was an outdoor pool behind the house. At first, with his view from above, Harry thought the children were just splashing around, but as he inched closer he overheard the conversation of the men who paced the poolside. One of them knelt down and took a small object from a little boy.

"Well retrieved, Shakespeare," he said. "See if you can do it again." He flicked the sparking object back into the pool, and the boy kicked away from the side and dived after it, narrowly avoiding two girls who were struggling to land a heavy picture frame.

"They're not bad, are they?" the man remarked to his companion, as they helped the girls with the frame. "When do they sail?"

"The *Amistad* leaves next week, so they'd better be ready, if they don't want to drown!" The picture frame crashed to the concrete, and he launched a torrent of abuse at the girls. One of them burst into tears.

"I'm cold!" she wailed. "Can I come out?"

"You'll be a lot colder at sea," he warned her. "Ten more lengths and you can come out."

The nature of Yakamoto's business dawned on Harry. These children must be unregistered. Bought children or stolen, like Cornubia's missing baby. They had nobody to mourn them if they drowned. He clutched the pen in his pocket and slowly withdrew the drone. It was level with the sleeping dog when a rough hand clamped down on his shoulder. He felt the cold bite of a blade against the nape of his neck.

"Who are you, and what are you doing here?"

Harry raised his hands, still clutching the thumb controller. "I'm Harry Van Basten," he said. "Van Basten, from Tent Town." At the repetition of the code, the drone should follow his programming and head straight for Ub-hot. Hopefully.

"Drop that, stand up, and turn around slowly. Keep your hands away from your Pod."

Harry knew with sinking certainty that his discoverer would be one of Yakamoto's goons. He turned, the unsheathed blade tickling his neck, to find two men glaring at him.

The man holding the sword spat. "Harry Van Basten, my arse. You're Muller. We heard you might be snooping around."

Harry spread his hands in a gesture of innocence. "I didn't even get as far as snooping! How about pretending you haven't seen me, and I won't dig any further into your boss's business. Sound fair?"

"Too late." The second man fiddled with his Pod. "Mr Yakamoto's on his way. He's livid with you."

"A man who uses unregistered children to retrieve sunken artefacts isn't someone I'm too fond of, either," Harry retorted. "That's what he's up to, isn't it?" From their silence, he knew he was right. "Come on, these are little kids! And the Drowned Lands are designated as a grave. You know this is wrong. Does he cut you a share of the profits in exchange for your silence?"

"Everyone knows about it," the swordsman muttered, the tip of his blade wavering a fraction. In the distance, approaching rapidly, Harry heard the buzz of the helicopter.

"Everyone knew about slavery, hundreds of years ago. Being aware of something makes it all right to ignore it, does it?" He had to raise his voice; the helicopter had arrived with incredible speed and now hovered directly overhead. Harry shielded his face from the fierce downdraft. The men strapped a harness around his body, and he was lifted from his feet. The webbing dug painfully into his armpits and crotch. By the time he was winched into the helicopter, it was more than whirling dust making his eyes water.

Yakamoto scowled at him, as the helicopter veered away from the Downs. "What a shame!" he shouted over the engine noise. "You should have listened to me. Cornubia wouldn't listen, either."

"What did you say to her?" The helicopter banked, and Harry clutched the seats to keep from falling.

"Cornubia knew the deal when she joined the *Amistad,* but she didn't want to give up her child. She foolishly ran away. I went to great trouble to get her back from the *Britain.*"

"Is that why you killed her? Because she caused you trouble?"

"She killed herself, Mr Muller."

"Don't give me that. I saw her body. She was slit right open."

"We were taking her to Scotland when she threw herself from the helicopter. As she hit the roof of the Circus, she must have become caught on a protruding piece of glass. A tragic accident."

"You're a sick man, Mr Yakamoto, sending children to do your grave-robbing for you."

"I find 'grave-robbing' an ugly phrase. Why shouldn't I make a profit from retrieving artefacts and selling them? I give those children a home and food out of the profits."

"Those that survive, you mean? Why little kids?"

"Grown men would demand too much money to dive into waters that are toxic with death. And children are small. They can reach places adults can't." He rose, moving sure-footed as the helicopter hovered. A red man pushed the door open. Glancing over his shoulder, Harry saw the glass dome of the Circus. The hum of the rotors disturbed the gulls feasting on Cornubia's body, and they rose in a great shrieking white cloud.

Yakamoto took a step towards him, a knife gleaming in his hand. "It's all about convenience, Mr Muller. You have made yourself inconvenient today. I warned you it could be painful."

Harry lashed out with his foot. The blade spun out of Yakamoto's hand, and the old man cursed. "Get him!"

Two of the red men leapt on Harry, wrestling him towards the open door, when a massive explosion sent the helicopter spinning. As it whirled, Harry caught a sickening glimpse of the *Great Britain,* sails billowing as she raced up the Haymarket. He clicked his Pod. "Victoria!"

"Harry! Where are you?"

"On the helicopter. What the hell was that?"

"A warning shot. Get out of there!"

"Where to?" But she had gone, and the thugs, regaining their feet, advanced on him. Harry, at the door, saw a puff of smoke rise from the *Britain's* deck, heard the report of the cannon. He had nowhere else to go. He jumped.

He crashed feet-first through the roof of the Circus, feeling the glass tear searing lines along both legs. Tangled with Cornubia's body, they fell together, slamming into the sun-warmed water and down, far into the chilly depths. Harry saw mannequins staring at him from sunken shop windows as, with a burst of adrenaline, he kicked free of Cornubia and back up towards the light. And then the sun exploded, a fireball of red and orange flame. Harry dived as the remaining glass shattered, raining down around him. There was nowhere to go but down, until his lungs burned as hard as the sky.

"Harry?" He heard Victoria's faint voice in his ear, but darkness gathered in his eyes, and it was impossible to answer.

* * *

Harry woke up in hospital, every limb bandaged and stinging. Victoria sat on his bed, eating grapes. *His* grapes, he was sure.

"Grapes are for sick people," he croaked. "Government rules."

"You're not sick," she replied, tartly. "Besides, Magda got you a whole seal, and the Dutch exiles gave a banquet in your honour. Too bad you missed it."

He tried to sit up without wincing and failed. "Yakamoto?"

"In a million bits, along with his helicopter. Those pirates are good shots. I wouldn't want to piss them off."

Harry groaned. "How did you get there so fast?"

"The *Britain* was coming to pick up Cornubia. I followed them and gave them the drone data you sent Infocon. When the helicopter turned up they weren't going to miss their chance to avenge Cornubia and save those kids. Don't blame them, either."

"The kids! Did they find the baby?"

"You mean this baby?" Berkley appeared in the doorway, holding the baby awkwardly. Victoria tutted.

"You're holding him like a sack of spuds," she chided. "Give him here." She offered him to Harry, who put his hands firmly behind his back. He was as clueless with babies as Berkley.

"Captain Cutler said I could bring him in to see you," Berkley said. "They're naming him Coran. Coran Harry Penhallow."

"Hell of a name, poor kid." But Harry smiled. With the pirates of the Cumberland Basin looking after him, Coran Harry Penhallow would grow up with nothing larger than his name to worry about.

THERMOCLINES
By
Colin Harvey

Lightning flashes in the distance, and fear rises like a bubble from the bottom of a stagnant pond. I flap my wings harder against the headwind I've been fighting since leaving the Irish Sea, but terror weighs my muscles down. If I hadn't left it so late and the wind hadn't picked up, I'd be home by now. If, if. If the wind hasn't swung round so I've flown past the village in the dark without realising.

When the rain hits, it'll weigh down my wings until I can no longer fly. You're going to die far from home, the fear says. You're going to ditch in the Grey; your lungs will fill with that burning smog, your skin will blister, your flesh bubble, and no one will know what happened to Garyn Jenkins.

"Bloody wind!" I shout with breath I can hardly spare. "*Bas*-tard rain! Bloody thermoclines! Bloody, bloody Grey!" Anger at the legacy of our ancestor's folly lends me fresh wind.

Then the darkness deepens enough for the candle-trees to ignite, lighting up the familiar valley ahead. As their fiery berries brighten, I shout with joy, and tears of relief half-blind me. The trees will burn for an hour, long enough for me to get home. Unless I hit a thermocline.

Tonight, though, I manage to avoid any of the lethal temperature inversions. By the time I reach Pembroke Trees, fear is a distant memory. Instead I think, I've flown at night and lived!

I dig my toenails into the bending branches of my favourite mountain-ash. The hand-sized berries of the candle-trees are still burning nearby, and I inhale their waxy scent. Not much smells in our empty, history-haunted ruin of a world, so I relish what there is. Tonight's berries have burnt to dust, scattering their seeds onto the wind, one of the few plants able to prosper in the world-wide lowland carpet of the Grey. Tomorrow night more will burn. Our forefathers who gengineered them weren't always foolish. They were clever sometimes, which only makes their idiocy greater.

The berries' cold phosphorescence casts patterns of shadow and light. My five-foot wings are still outstretched—I've been flying so long they've cramped open—and I slowly furl them. Old Thom tells us that we look like what our ancestors called angels. "If," he says, "angels had feathers all over their body from the Adam's Apple downwards."

I call into the slowly fading light, "Who's Adam? And what's an apple?"

A chuckle comes from the darkness. Rhodri says from the branch below, "I dunno!" Anger rises from beneath his laughter. "I thought you wasn't going to make it!"

I'm shaking with fatigue, but I laugh. I'm not going to let him know how scared I was. "No problem; I'd have just nested in a tree."

"You'd have missed them, if you had." Smugness stains his voice. "We have two guests. Father and daughter."

What? A woman travelling, almost alone? But I don't let my astonishment show. He won't hear *me* get excited. "Best go to dinner, then," I say. I launch into the air and flap hard. Our wings are great for soaring on thermals but bugger-all use for tree hopping.

"Okaay!" He whoops.

Rhodri and I are contra-twins. He's as fair as I'm dark, outgoing to my quiet; thin compared to me, though I'm solid, not fat. We've been friends all our lives, but always known that with Emily, the only girl our age in the village, one of us will have to leave or look elsewhere to marry. Maybe both, if she chooses surly Rob instead. Rob's a year older than us, and he thinks he's our better. So we avoid him, and he ignores us. Whatever happens, though we try to ignore it, we know that once Emily starts to bleed, our friendship is history.

I stop at our hut, swaying at the top of Tree Six. I unclip the fishing net on the end of a pole slung over my shoulder, and my goody-bag with today's haul: three eggs filched from a gull's nest, despite flapping wings and savage beaks, and two sea-bass. Not much for twelve hours flying. Winters are even harder.

Then I fly to the galley platform.

In the evenings, we eat Jacama fruit and leaves from the upside-down trees and in a good season, meat, even though prey is rare as a woman and as hard to catch. Myfanwy cooks with herbs grown in one of her little window-pots, so pigeon or gull never tastes the same way twice.

When we've eaten we swap the day's news. Afterwards Old Thom tells stories of when the land was a green carpet, and men built metal towers to the sky. How the Ancients remade themselves in all shapes and forms, just because they could. I can swallow the idea of Wingless men—but fish-men? Old Thom says that's because when mankind went Upaloft to the stars, they took fish-men with them to settle water-worlds. We just laugh at that, which makes Old Thom snort with disgust. Young Thom sits and drools, showing even true-genes can breed false. When we're done, we head to our nests for the night.

Tonight's different. Instead I hover outside, tired wings taking long, slow strokes unheard against the other's chatter. But what sounds close to an argument cuts through the talk. "There's more than one kind of superstition." The stranger's voice is a rook-like caw. "Were-birds, mutants, Others." He snorts. "We haven't yet devolved to thinking the world's flat, but once I was in a village that thought the sun orbited the Earth. We're sliding backwards to barbarism, I tell you."

Twenty-eight heads turn as I enter the platform, looking for our first guests in three years. The next village is Abergwan, thirty miles away and twice our size; here at the western end of the world, travellers are rare but encouraged.

"Garyn. You made it." I can't tell if Da's annoyed. He rarely shows emotion.

"Sorry I'm late," I say. "I was fishing off Skomer Island, and I hit another thermocline. Ended up in the water for a few seconds. Had to sit on a rock 'til I dried off." I didn't need to tell him how nearly I'd skirted death. "Lucky the Grey don't go over the water. I lost time trying to see if I could find the fish I was after. He was a big bugger."

"You let *boys* fish out to sea?" The stranger's voice cuts across us. The implications of what I said sink in, and he adds hurriedly, "Even a boy who survives a thermocline."

Old Thom answers for Da, and his tone brooks no argument: "He's young, Mordechai, but Garyn is the best flyer in Wales." I'm amazed. I had no idea Old Thom thought me good for anything.

"My apologies," Mordechai says, "I meant no offence."

"It's *because* he's so young that he has survived." Da adds, "As we get older, our reflexes slow."

"We need judgement, not reflexes," Mordechai fires back. "A grown man would know to steer clear of taking risks."

"No risk, no reward!" Da's getting annoyed. "We never used to be able to regain control after hitting a thermocline. It was Garyn showed us how to level out of the fall that bit faster. Six or more of us owe our lives to him."

Embarrassed, I don't add that I've survived almost a dozen of them—that would be bragging. Instead, I shuffle, to get a better look at Mordechai. He's red-bearded above his throat, red-feathered below. He's big and strong but with a harsh look that hints at cruelty. He studies me.

Then I see his daughter and bow, blushing.

They're both wearing the same plain blue coveralls as us. Perhaps she takes after her Ma, rather than him. Dark haired, with white skin blending into white feathers, she's delicate enough to blow away in a breeze. Her look cuts right through me, and my cheeks burn. My heart is thumping fiercer than when I nearly plummeted into the sea.

I hop over to my perch, suddenly conscious of how awkward we are on the ground. Myfanwy brings a platter to me and one for Rhodri. Her feet are like oval plates compared to our clawed ones and only arms sprout from her single shoulder-sockets, but for all that she's a freak (Old Thom claims she's like First Humans), she's better on a flat surface than us.

She puts my platter on the lectern in front of me. I stare at it. "Tree squirrel? Is it a feast day?" She fills my glass and chucks me under what she says passes for my chin, and I pull away, heat rising to my face. She reckons that once everyone had a chin as big as hers. "Lantern-tree wine, not water?" I look at the pale yellow-liquid in delight. "All my dreams are coming true!"

"Not all," she says. "Not yet, surely?" She nods at our visitor with a little smile. "Her name is Kazia." She changes the subject: "I thought you were going to take it easy after the last thermocline." She puts her hand on her broad hip and thrusts out that eye-popping featherless cleavage. "Remember?"

Of course. How can I forget? I'd swooped low after a pigeon, ignoring my itching skin and the warning prickle in my nostrils. Brushing cold air beneath warm, I fell so far, so fast, I almost landed in the Grey; it smelt of puke, and even though I only had a sniff, I was still sick enough to need Myfanwy's herbs.

She'd clucked maternally. "Few would've noticed such a small thermocline at all," she'd said. "Old Thom says the word *thermocline* used to be used about water, not air." She laughed. "You know what he's like. What he doesn't know I think he makes up." She sobered. "But you were lucky."

She taps my shoulder on her way back. "Stop staring," she says. "First time I've ever seen men concentrate on anything." She adds, "They've been trying to get him to leave the girl here, before they wandered off the subject as usual."

We watch them like we're waiting for cliff-rats. Patient, unwavering. Mordechai matches us, making sure when he looks away that we know he chooses to, not because we've forced it. When *I* look away from him, it's to find Kazia studying me, equally unwavering, and I feel my face burn again.

I catch Emily watching me. Her normally ruddy face is almost as white as Kazia's, but it's a death white, and she's close to tears. I harden my heart.

We strain to hear every single word of news they bring. Tonight's feast will dent our supplies, but so what? We sit silent as Old Thom and Mordechai exchange tall tales of the Old Days and Mankind's flight to the stars. For all his supposed cleverness, Old Thom has never been able to say why our great-grandfathers didn't go Upaloft, and there are as many theories why as people in the village. That we're descendants of a splinter group who refused to go; our ship crashed on its way to pick us up; or our Grand-Da's committed some terrible crime for which they were left behind; even that mankind never went Upaloft at all, and we're the last humans. Old Thom hems and haws, showing how useless learning is.

"Aye," Mordechai grunts. "They never thought of those they abandoned on the margins." He says brightening, "I've heard of communities on the continent. That in the highest mountains the Grey isn't a problem, even in the valleys between the hills, and that they can even grow food in the ground. One day they might even regain the stars."

We bite our lips to hide our smiles at such foolishness. Our lives aren't about regaining the stars, just survival.

But our self-control breaks when Mordechai brags of having visited Brisel. "Aye, I've seen the Necropolis," he says. "Black towers piercing the sky, haunted by Deadwalkers and cannibals. Barely got away with our kidneys."

"Bull-*shit!*" Rhodri mutters. They glare at him, and he falls silent.

"I've always known Brisel as the first of the flying cities," Old Thom says, not wanting to call our guest a liar but unable to swallow this latest fancy. "Never heard of any city of the dead."

"It was the last, too," Mordechai says. "Or it would've been, had it flown. But something happened at a place called Canesh'm, something that left thousands dead and their ghosts haunting the place."

Old Thom doesn't flat out call him a liar but looks sceptical.

At the end of the evening they stand. For the first time, I realise just how big Mordechai is. "He must be almost five foot three!" I hiss at Rhodri.

He pitches his voice in an impersonation of Old Thom's sepulchral sing-song: "In the old days they was bigger still...gi-ants, they was, I tell you, boy. Six feet tall!"

"No-oo," I add in my own parody. "Eight!"

We collapse into giggles, then catch Da and Mervyn — Rhodri's Da—glaring at us. I grow serious. With his huge pectorals, Mordechai is a flying barrel. "How much do you reckon he weighs?" I murmur.

Rhodri shrugs, and murmurs back, "A hundred pounds?"

I whistle. That's with our hollow bones. Old Thom has Myfanwy give us a biology lesson every time someone dies. He's so stuck in the past, he's desperate we won't lose any of his precious learning—as if it will put food in our bellies.

Myfanwy cutting Gregory open, working quickly before the man's body could begin to decay, before the Grey could wreak such havoc it would make the carcass unrecognizable and waste an anatomy lesson. Showing us blistered skin and oozing pus, the legacy of just a few seconds in the Grey, she pointed at something almost hidden by the gore. "That's an extra-long trachea—windpipe to you. It folds up accordion-style, and inflates with air during long flights." I was too busy trying not to lose my breakfast to ask what an accordion was, but I got her meaning. We're built for flight...

Still...

"He must struggle to fly very far," I say.

"They flew over the Severn Sea," Rhodri whispers, as they approach.

"Flew, or floated like a big gasbag?" I ask.

They pass, and Mordechai purses his lips as he sees Myfanwy. "A Wingless?" His tone is studiedly neutral.

"She's a good cook and a better healer," Da says. The shame in his voice makes me want to shout at them.

"And good for comforting widowers and virgins?" Mordechai asks. Realising he may have given offence, he adds, "Not all villages are so tolerant of deviants. It does you credit."

"It's easy to mistake that tolerance for softness," Da says quietly, the warning clear. He adds, affably, "Do think about marrying Kazia to one of our boys, won't you?"

Mordechai finally says: "What if we stay a week? We've found that places that seem alright at first aren't always so good when you dig deeper." He holds up a placating hand. "I'm not suggesting that it's the case here, but we can't be too careful. One village, it turned out that they clipped their women's wings—to keep 'em safe, they said."

I'm shocked. Our women have always hunted, if in pairs in case of raids. Old Thom says, "The girls fly here until they're too pregnant. We need food as much as babies."

We almost fall over each other to escort them to Kern's nest. He'll share with the Thoms while they stay. Mordechai bows his gratitude. "This'd be a fine place to stay for good, if I didn't want so badly to see the truth of the legends. I've heard the crossing over the great bridge to the continent is a hard one. But we'll stay a week. It'll give me a chance to meet my future son-in-law."

When the older men have gone Mordechai bids us goodnight, adding, "You boys won't pester my girl. If you wish to court her, you'll do so through me. I'll decide a week from now. The *men* have agreed this."

As we turn away, Kazia's hand brushes mine, and she speaks for the first time, in a low voice. "May I ask their names, Father?"

Mordechai grunts.

We introduce ourselves, Rob clearly making an effort, Rhodri gallantly, me woodenly. I wish I had Rhodri's ease with her. She shakes my hand, brushing her thumb back and forth as she does so, then wishes us goodnight. As they turn away she whispers, "Later," to me.

We fly back to the others, Rhodri so preoccupied he barely taunts me when I plead a headache and go to bed early. I clamber into my nest and sit in the dark, my head whirling. She wants to meet me? She wants to meet me!

My father returns, finding me sitting in the dark. He's brought a candle-shrub for light and studies me. "You're smitten, hey?" He smiles. "Poor Emily. Suddenly she's no longer the centre of the world."

I shrug. "She can still choose who she wants here or pick a husband at the Summer Fair. She'll live."

"Mordechai'll drive a hard bargain." Da chuckles. "You'll need more than a talent for catching food and a few tree-sculptures to win her."

"I know." I sigh. She might prefer me, but it will be Mordechai's choice. What can I offer that he'd want?

I say I need some air, and go outside.

* * *

She makes me wait, but eventually the branch shakes, and she's beside me. She has a smell, no, a fragrance I've never known before. Her shoulder's warm against mine. She snuggles closer. "There aren't many women here," she says, chatting.

"Rhodri's Ma died bearing him," I explain. "Couldn't cope with the size of his wings. Mine died when I was three, falling into the Grey in a storm." I'm gabbling. I shut up.

She says, "Are you and Rhodri best mates?"

"Aye. We learnt to fly at the same time."

She comes even closer. "My father will kill us if he finds us," she whispers. That just makes it more exciting. When she touches me, it feels as if the earth—or the tree— shakes.

"So why *are* we here?" I tease. I feel her lips press mine, and then her tongue flicks into my mouth. I put my arms round her.

"You know why." Her hands are everywhere. "It's *you* I want. But we need to convince *him*." I stifle a moan as she strokes me. "When we're married," she whispers, "I want

163

babies. But 'til then I must be a good girl. So it's hands and mouths only."

The branch below us shakes. It *was* the tree that moved. "There you are, you little tramp!" Mordechai's rumble makes her shiver in my hands. Then it's our branch that rocks.

I shield her. "Don't blame her!"

"You." He leans into my face. His breath smells. "Had best be *very* careful, young man. If you go near my daughter again, you're out. Understand?"

I nod, and they're gone. It's all happened so quickly and quietly that no one's heard.

Later, I lie in bed thinking of her. In the night I hear a cry that might have come from her tree but might just as easily be a wild thing calling in the darkness.

* * *

For three days I quarter the hunting grounds, flying in golden sunshine that alternates with sweeping curtains of rain, Kazia's presence hovering beside me like her fragrance.

Once I fly over the metal forest of the Old Docks, where ships came from all over the world to discharge vast lakes of petrochemicals. Normally I avoid the place, but today I can even smile on the rusting towers and gigantic pipes. Below me, even the Grey—accidental spillage or a botched experiment—seems less sinister.

Usually only the highest peaks can poke through the oily sheen hovering a few inches above the ground. But for once, I see a few abandoned slate quarries. Moss and lichens—among the few things that can resist the Grey— decorate the blue slate in a bouquet of greens and yellows.

Da and me rack our brains every night for things to interest Mordechai. We raid Da's hoard, carefully garnered over many years from treasure grounds. Da's crumbling dictionary is one I can't read, but I love the sound of words, and use 'em when I can, so his treasures are garnered, not gathered: what Da says is a timepiece that straps to a man's wrist; a tube with a light that shines when I push a button; a counting machine, dead now, but we only need a couple of little power cells to make it work. And as much food as we can muster.

Every night Kazia and Mordechai are surrounded, so I can't get her alone. When I catch her watching me, her expression's unreadable.

On the third evening Mordechai announces his choice.

We've done as best we can, but it's not enough. Rhodri will wed Kazia next week. Mordechai thanks us for our offer.

Rhodri mutters, "Sorry," as he passes, but he's grinning, and I know he's no sorrier than I'd be, if we'd won.

I shrug Da's consoling arm off and go to my suddenly lonely bed. Our dowry will be returned tomorrow morning.

* * *

But next morning, Da shakes me awake. "They've fled!" In the candlelight he looks old, shrunken. "They've taken as much as they can carry!" He almost sobs. "Rob's compass and a whole sackful of food. Thieving bandits!"

In the galley, people mill round like mobbing gulls. "They've done this before," Rhodri says bitterly. He looks as shattered as I feel. "They was too well organised."

I wonder if Kazia hugged him, as well. And Rob? I hope not. But it'd be a good way to inflate the dowries.

Young Thom shakes his head. "I almost begged them to stay," he wails.

Da claps his shoulder. "He got you thinking it was your idea." He tries to comfort the old man. "Like Rhodri says, they've done this before."

We gather, claws skittering on the wooden floor of the dining galley. Rhodri, Mervyn, Da, and me. Rob and Hywel, his Da. Mort, two years younger than Rhodri and me, barely old enough for man's work. Caspar, his wife seven months pregnant. Christian, only a few years older than us, but already married with bairns. One-eyed Jack. Kern. Big, burly flyers all. Only frail Old Thom and his drooling offspring will stay behind.

"They'll have a head start," Old Thom says. "But they'll be weighed down with their haul," he adds.

We each take our pole with the fishing net on the end, and strap it over our shoulder. We put a firework in the goody-bag that we'll sling across the other shoulder, and a handful of sugary melon-berries and some Jacama fruit. I strap a water bottle to my waist. Apart from that we carry nothing and wear little.

Outside, the sky turns orange with the sunrise.

"What happens when we catch 'em?" Rhodri asks. His white face tells me he knows the answer. Rage fills me at the way our hospitality's been abused.

"Take the girl alive if you can," Old Thom says. "We'll breed from her once we've clipped her wings. She's his accomplice, after all. If not, kill her as well."

Da nods. "Mordechai dies," he says. "We'll hang his body from the trees and let the carrion birds feast."

"Then we'll catch the carrion birds and eat them," Rob says. "At least some good'll come of this mess then. And if anyone else comes a-visiting, they'll see what happens to thieves."

I try not to think of eating birds that've fed on human flesh. It's too close to cannibalism. We've never had to do that.

But it's as it should be. I drown any thoughts of mercy in an ocean of bile. It's coloured grey.

* * *

We flap aloft and seek the first thermals. We'll circle round the village in ever-widening spirals. Whoever finds them will fire their flare for the others to follow.

I think otherwise: Mordechai gave us a clue when he mentioned the Europa Bridge. I've no desire to make myself look more a fool than I have already, so I'll go alone. I can fly farther and faster than anyone in the village.

I climb higher, wings beating slowly. As the heat of the day grows, I soar higher on outstretched wings, still circling the village. My lungs ache from drawing in the thin air, and my ears pop. They must have left at night, and I imagine lifting-off in the dark, the desperate silence, the effort it took to beat their wings in long, hard, regular strokes with no assistance from thermals.

Squinting, I see two specks in the distant east.

I bare my teeth and give chase.

* * *

There's a tailwind up here, and all morning I reel them in. When I tire I gobble some melon-berries. But it's anger that really fuels me. If I don't use it, it'll eat me from inside.

By noon, I'm almost above them. I grip the net under my arm, turning it into a spear. I furl my wings, swooping into a steep dive.

The wind buffets me as I close on them, and I'm unsure whether the roaring in my ears is the wind or my blood pounding. I come from above and out of the sun, so Mordechai never sees me. I hit him so hard that the impact tears the spear from my grasp, leaving splinters in my arm.

He plummets to the ground, to make a twisted scarlet mess among the tendrils of the Grey. So much for hanging his carcass. I nearly end up with him, but manage to pull out just in time.

Ignoring the pain from the splinters, I pursue Kazia, climbing slowly. She flies as if pursued by all the Deadwalkers of hell.

We fly on and on: I almost catch her, and she dives northwards. I overhaul her, and she turns back east, then south, then east again. She dropped her booty when I hit Mordechai, so we're flying equally light, but I reel her in gradually each time.

Eventually, as the sun sinks low behind us, I'm within shouting distance of her. But she calls first, weakly, gasping for breath. "Let me go! I'm dead without Mordechai, so you've had your revenge!"

"You reckon?" I snarl, but it's half-hearted. Killing Mordechai has lanced the boil of my hatred. I only pity her now and their shabby little trick.

"You judge us?" she says. "You in your smug little world! Fly home *boy!* Go back to your fishing! You don't know how hard it is to survive outside your precious village!"

"Then make it easier!" I shout back. "Come back with us, and we'll let you live! We need children more than we need revenge!"

"Tell Mordechai that!" She dives southwards, catching me by surprise.

I gobble the last of my berries. We cross a huge river that narrows upstream, eastwards, so I guess it's the Brisel Channel.

We reach land again. The Grey is thicker than ever. I reel her in, metre by metre, then a centimetre at a time. I can only wonder at her stamina. I'm fit, but I'm ready to drop. It seems criminal to clip her wings — if I can take her alive.

Occasionally the Grey parts, to reveal outlines in the ground, as if something had been there once. Faint squares, thousands of them, imprinted in the ground.

I see trees in the distance. Did she know they were here? I have to catch her before we reach them or she might escape again. If I can fly in the dark, so can she.

I fly harder, faster, toward the trees, digging into reserves of strength I didn't know I had, heading her off. I wobble a little as I pass over her. I know the *exact* moment she realises her escape's cut off because her flight path, until now spear-straight, wavers.

Ahead of me in the distance is a vast black pit.

"Do you know where you are, *boy*?" Kazia calls.

"Doesn't matter," I say. "Give up, Kazia."

"That's Canesh'm," she says. "The black pit is the remains of the flying city that exploded on take-off."

"If the legends are true—it could be natural." It sounds lame, even to me. The pit glows slick and black and evil in the twilight.

We hover, wings fluttering in the wind. She doesn't even bother to answer my suggestion, instead says, "I wanted to visit so many places: the Europa Bridge, the Fens...Oh well, I guess that's as much as I get to see." Her wings still, then she plummets. "I'd rather be dead than a Wingless baby-machine!"

It's like I hit a thermocline in my head. My fall from anger matches her fall from the sky. My rage is used up, or maybe I've been won over by her. She mustn't die like this. It's too wasteful.

I furl my wings tight, and dive.

She's a couple of hundred feet below me. The wind tugs my cheeks into a snarl. Gravity's vice-tight grip squeezes my head.

I've never thought about it before, but if you survive a thermocline, you always see things differently after. I realise that she's no whore, just desperate. Maybe Mordechai was once young and brave, before desperation corrupted him?

She's getting closer, only a few yards from me now.

We live in little bubbles of loneliness like Pembroke Trees, only meeting outsiders at the seasonal fairs. Only the brides we barter move between villages. We become more alike in our thoughts, more inbred.

There are other villages that need to learn to survive falling from a thermocline.

I can't see anything except Kazia, tumbling end over end toward the Grey, which fills my vision. I can smell its stink.

Right now anything seems possible. I hold out my arm, stretching, straining every tendon. "Grab my hand!" I shout. "We'll head for the trees!"

I feel a thermocline's prickling.

She's only inches from me...I can almost reach her...I manage to grab a wing, my other hand and a foot clutching desperately onto her cold arm, and I hear a ripping sound—a muscle? I dare not ease my grip. *Concentrate, Garyn,* I think. *Open your wings, boy! Slow your dive!*

I smell and taste and feel the slimy, burnt sickness that is the Grey. My shoulders strain to near-dislocation. My lungs heaving, I stop.

Then slowly haul her up.

What will her exposure to the Grey do? What if she's brain-dead? *Worry about that later, mate. For the moment she's safe.*

Her breathing has stopped. I carry her back to a lone Jacama tree amid the oaks, my foot screaming in agony. I rest her in the crook of two branches like the Indoos that Old Thom said hung their dead from platforms. Only she's not dead yet. Not if I've anything to do with it.

I pound on her chest, the way Myfanwy showed us at home, and she coughs. I sit awkwardly in the bole, cradling her head in my arm.

I sleep. The last thing I see before I drift off is something moving, in the Grey. Eyes. Probably my imagination—or a dream.

* * *

I awake in the morning, cold and stiff. This one Jacama tree is stunted and its fruit sparse, but it's home as far as I'm concerned. Kazia vomited in the night, but I was so tired I slept through it. I rage at myself as I wipe the nasty pink froth off her lips. I've seen this before; men coughing their guts up. Her body's so hot to the touch that it almost burns me. I wipe her down with my hand, which I've rinsed with water from my bottle. We can survive on Jacama berries, but their juice is sticky. To save water I eat Jacama berries and spit their liquid into her mouth.

The day is grey, like the murk at the foot of the tree. For the first time in maybe my whole life I have nothing to do but think and no one to distract me.

I wonder why the Grey only affects animals—most plants seem unaffected, while no one knows about insects. Were our Great-Grand-Da's punishing us?

When I've worried such thoughts to death, I try to work out what it was that I saw the night before, assuming it was real. Maybe animals can survive the Grey, here in the empty spaces between villages away from hunters. They'd need to be simple creatures, snakes or suchlike. Not mammals, which never survive the Grey.

Kazia cries out several times that day. Sometimes her sobs sound almost like words. Occasionally she grunts, and once she laughs, the dirtiest sound I've heard in a while, and I wonder about her life before. Whether she really was his daughter...

In the afternoon she vomits pink stuff again, and when I try to force water down her throat, she coughs it up. But she hasn't breathed in as much as others. She doesn't die, and I wonder at the resilience in such a small body. Perhaps she might somehow, by a miracle, make it. More likely it's simply the false dawn before death.

No one's ever lived this long after breathing in the Grey. We've tried everything at Pembroke Trees. Surgery, fluids, feeding, starving—nothing works. At least she'll be spared Myfanwy's knife, which usually cuts into the corpse's flesh within the hour, before the body can rot.

Night begins to fall: I see movement in the Grey. There are eyes, again.

"Look at that, Kazia!" I leap from the tree, but it's gone before I can reach where it was. Only some sort of scuttling something, but the first life I've ever seen on the ground.

I return to my watch and realise that she's stopped breathing. I rip her top off, exposing flawless little feathered breasts that point at the evening sky. *No time for that now!* I pound her chest and breathe air into her mouth. She coughs, and I taste blood.

She spasms and sits bolt upright, and I recoil from the almost blackness of her oversized irises. The Grey is not only eating her inside, but changing her in other ways as well. "Garyn," she croaks, then falls into my arms. I want to weep and shout with joy at the same time, but all I can do is hold her, and mumble nothings. Her eyes have shut again, and I lean her back gently into the crook of the branches.

I sit until long after nightfall before sleeping again.

* * *

It's still night, a fat moon hanging yellow over the skyline. I listen, trying to work out what's woken me.

Silence all around. Not even the sound of Kazia's breathing. I try to rouse her, but though I pound on her chest until her ribs must surely crack, and blow into her mouth, there's no response. Sobbing, I cradle her body in my arms.

I can only grieve so much and as daybreak stains the east, despite my swollen eyes, I sleep again.

* * *

I awake cold and stiff. Kazia lies where I allowed her to fall into the crook of the branches. She's still soft to the touch. No sign of Rigor yet.

"I wish I'd known you better," I say. I am reluctant to leave her to the carrion birds. She's all that I have.

It is the loneliest, longest day of my life, and eventually I curl up around Kazia's cooling body and sleep.

* * *

The next morning, I know I must leave, but still don't feel ready. As if taunting me, the day is warm, the sun fighting its way through dull grey streamers of clouds scudding on the wind.

Kazia's body is warm where I have lain against it, and I kiss her cool lifeless lips. I know she'd mock me as still a boy, but I don't care. I love her, see?

Her skin is turning iridescent, and I wonder what evil the bastard Grey is still working on her. Soon, I suppose, she'll start to moulder. I should leave her now, while she still looks as she did in life. But I'm reluctant. I'm almost convinced that I see her chest rise and fall faintly, and she's still warm-ish.

I remember Myfanwy cutting open Gregory to expose giant internal air sacs and his heart—as large as my head—beneath his protruding breastbone, and I'm glad I won't have to see Kazia like that, but guilty too that I'll lose that valuable knowledge.

I prepare to leave.

"Garyn." Kazia's whisper almost makes me fall out of the tree in shock. She moves. It's only a tiny shudder, but it's movement, not the involuntary twitch of a corpse.

I leap on her, cackling. "What? How? How did?"

Eventually, I stop gibbering and lean back and grin at her.

She opens strange eyes with huge black irises, smiles faintly, and coughs. She wriggles into a more comfortable position and winces. "My chest hurts," she says. "Have you been hitting me?"

"Every hour." My cheeks hurt from the width of my grin. "Tried to keep you breathing." She's deathly cold.

"Maybe that wasn't what was needed," she whispers, but smiles. I feel suddenly shy. "I dreamt that you were holding me," she says.

"I did. Fed you, and wiped the puke off." I shake my head. "How did you survive?"

"I dunno." She frowns, concentrating. "What was different? What didn't you do, or do, that the others didn't?"

"The others all died; we dissected them—"

"Before they could be affected by the Grey." She sits upright so violently that she almost falls out of the tree. "How long did I lie there?"

I shake my head. "Three days...I think." I swallow, bile acrid in my throat. "I let you die. I slept, while—"

She puts a finger to my lips. "You kept me warm for long enough then let me die so that I might live." Her kiss is only a peck on my cheek, but I still stir. "And you kept me warm, while the Grey worked on me."

"Worked how?" I squint at her. What's she turned into?

"I'm starving," she says, ignoring me. The sun sends streamers of light through the clouds, and she stretches her wings out wide. The sunlight glints off her now iridescent skin, and she shuts her eyes and smiles. "I'm feeding on sunlight." She laughs, bemused. "All this time we thought the Grey was poisonous, it was there to change us." She looks at me. "I think I can still eat food, but this is like a back-up system." She tears off a couple of leaves, and munches them. "Delicious," she mumbles around a mouthful, but she grimaces. I try one and spit it out. She giggles. "Useful in an emergency. Maybe the taste grows on you."

"If people knew about this..." I breathe.

"People." Kazia's face falls. "What now?"

"I dunno." I laugh, but without real humour. "All I could think of was keeping you alive—"

"So you could take me prisoner?"

I shake my head. "I hoped, that you...that I might..." I look away, blushing.

She lifts my chin. "I'm not sure I count as human any more."

I look her in the eye. "I don't care." I swallow. Then blurt, "I love you. I loved you in Pembroke Trees, and—"

She silences me with a kiss, gentle at first, then growing more passionate.

When we come up for air, she says, "I haven't changed that much, then..." Despite the darkness of her eyes, I still see laughter in them. Then they widen.

I turn around.

Two wingmen approach and hover about twenty metres away. Their skin is iridescent like hers—they're naked but for a loin-cloth each—and from what I can see, their eyes are as dark.

The smaller of them calls out, "The girl's one of us. She comes with us."

"I can't fly," Kazia says. "I'm still recovering."

"I'll carry her," I say. "I nursed her. She's my wife."

"You incubated her?" the small one cries.

"You're young to be married," the big one says in a surprisingly reedy voice.

"Don't matter," I say.

"Are you sure?" Kazia whispers. "Husband?"

"I had to say something," I whisper back. "Call it a statement of intent." I hoist her into my arms and almost fall from the ground when I leap from the tree.

"I'll help," the big one says.

The two strangers don't look too happy, but they set off ahead of us.

* * *

As we rise, I see the shapes of other wingmen in the distance. They look as if they're converging on us.

"What are those lines?" Kazia asks Nico, the smaller of the two, pointing to the too-regular ridges, and the imprints in the ground visible from above. "They're everywhere."

"They're the imprints of the city," he answers. "Where their buildings rested. This was Brisel, the first of the flying cities."

We skirt the evil-looking Canesh'm Crater and head up a valley even thicker with the Grey than usual. I comment on it.

"Stockwood Vale, on the edge of Brisel City," the second—unnamed—flyer grunts. That's all the explanation he gives, as if it should be enough.

I see trees at the top of the Vale. A half-dozen Beeches, Jacama, and an Ash, all thick with wingmen, I see as we close on them. All like Kazia and Nico.

"*This* is the Necropolis?" I gasp and start to laugh at the way truth is twisted by story. There are shapes moving in the mist, it parts long enough to reveal an animal, and then a wingman rises from the Grey. They seem at ease with it. That alone makes them more alien than anything else could.

"*This* is Whitchurch Trees," Nico says severely. "Our hatchery and our home. You savages wouldn't understand. We've learned to keep our distance from your kind."

"I'm sorry," I say. "I didn't mean to be rude." He seems to accept my apology.

We place Kazia in a Mountain Ash so like mine at home that I feel a pang of homesickness. An old voice that sounds just like Old Thom but with a different accent calls, "What've you brought us then, Nico?"

"Found one of us over at Bris," Nico says. "But she's married." He jerks a thumb at me. "He incubated her. We owe him, however we feel 'bout his kind."

"Well, I'll be buggered!" "Old Thom" says. "We may owe you, but you can't stay here, youngster. Not unless you'm prepared to take the dive."

"Hold!" Kazia cries. "How do we know it'll work for Garyn?"

"We know," Nico says. "Trial and error. It works for young 'uns, and the strong." He shrugs. "Maybe they meant it to work for everyone, but time was scarce and they cocked it up. Or not. Why waste it on the old or damaged?"

I gaze at the Grey, feel my palms grow clammy. My heart pounds. "I can't," I say. "In time, maybe..." I take a deep breath. I'm not sure I'll *ever* be ready, but I can't say that here.

"You can't stay here," someone else calls. "We won't have no savages!"

"Then I'll go."

Kazia touches my arm. "I won't be told what to do by strangers." She rocks backward and forward, worrying at the problem. I've never seen the girls at home like this, thinking, planning—except about food and babies. I like it.

"Give us two minutes to talk?" she calls out, and "Old Thom" nods.

But instead, she flies to the Jacama trees, grabbing handfuls of berries. Then onto the Beeches, where she rips something off. Then she flaps back, already looking stronger. The sunshine must be doing her good.

"Do you love me?" she whispers.

"You know I do!"

"Can we have children?"

I grin, slowly. "Dunno. We'll just have to practice."

"But not here."

She turns to the assembled crowd. "You need a second site, so you're not so vulnerable to attack."

"We knows that!" someone shouts. "But we can't spare people!"

I realise what she's planning and shout, "You can spare one girl you didn't know existed this morning."

Kazia calls, "I've taken Beech nuts and Jacama berries. We'll plant them at Bris. We'll be your second site."

There's an explosion of voices, but she turns to me. "I'm probably not fit enough to fly all the way back, but I can always rest, while you carry on or wait for me. Are you ready? Husband?"

"I'm ready," I say.

"Then let's re-seed Brisel."

The old and the new, human and post-human, we launch ourselves from the tree into the future.

What Would Nicolas Cage Have Done?

By Gareth L Powell

i.

On Monday morning, while sitting on the overcrowded eight o'clock bus from Portishead to Bristol, I decided to skip work. Michelle and I had split up the day before, and I really didn't feel like going into the office. Instead, I got off at the top of Rownham Hill and used my mobile phone to call in sick. Then I walked over the Suspension Bridge into Clifton. It was a cold, grey day and I needed some time to myself.

I bought a newspaper and sat on a park bench in a Georgian square with black railings, thinking things over and trying to figure out where and when our relationship had gone wrong. We'd been together a year and a half but now she was seeing someone else.

We'd broken up over a bottle of wine in a crowded bar by the river.

I'd said, "So that's it?"

She'd shrugged. "I guess so."

She'd fiddled with the stem of her glass, looking uncomfortable and upset. It was Sunday lunchtime and the place smelled of garlic and stale beer. There was nothing more to say. We finished the wine in silence and then went our separate ways.

Thinking about it now made me feel hollow and lonely. There was a cold wind blowing, and I was glad I had a warm jacket over my shirt and tie.

Most of the houses in the square had been converted into offices and flats. Some had dream catchers and rainbow stickers in their upper windows. Finding no answers there, I got up and walked along Pembroke Road to the Roman Catholic cathedral.

I stood looking at it from the opposite side of the road. Flanked on both sides by large, conservative town houses, its modern design and jagged, arty spires seemed out of place, and its concrete steps were slick with rain.

Turning my back on it, I cut through a side street that took me to Whiteladies Road—a busy main street lined with shops, galleries, restaurants, and bars—coming out by the building that used to be the old cinema.

I thought a bit of retail therapy might cheer me up, so I spent a few minutes flicking through the DVD bargain racks in Sainsbury's and bought a lottery ticket at the tobacco counter. Then, at around eleven o'clock, I walked out and up to the little bookshop on the hill, where I spent an hour browsing the shelves.

I loved that shop. It was small and independent and spread over several levels. There were leaflets and flyers stuck to the walls and the solid wooden floors creaked gently as I moved. There were potted plants on the windowsills, and the whole place had the relaxed atmosphere of a library.

I picked up a book I'd been meaning to read for a while. As I paid for it, the girl on the stool behind the till gave me a smile. I'd seen her in there before. She had long blonde hair, a short denim skirt, and tan cowboy boots.

"Good choice," she said. She slipped the book into a paper bag and handed it to me, and I thanked her. She pushed her hair back with one hand. There were silver bangles on her wrist.

"It's very good," she said.

A lorry went past the window. I said, "Have you read it, then?"

"I've read all his books. Well, the recent ones anyway. And this is definitely the best."

She had a dog-eared paperback on the counter in front of her, with a bus ticket sticking out of it in place of a bookmark.

"What's that you've got there?" I said.

She glanced down. "This?" She held the book up. It was a Penguin translation of the *Iliad*.

"Ah. I remember the first time I read that."

"You do?"

"I studied classics at college."

She sat up and brushed a strand of hair behind her ear. "Really?"

Her eyes flicked to the clock on the wall by the door. She said, "Look, I'm going for lunch in a minute. I don't suppose you'd like to...?"

Her legs were brown, and her eyes were blue, with little copper flecks. I hesitated for a second, thinking of Michelle and her new boyfriend. Then I smiled and said, "Yes. Yes, I'd like that very much."

* * *

Ten minutes later, we were sitting at a table in the window of a coffee house near Clifton Down shopping centre. My new friend insisted on paying for the drinks. She had a cup of tea with lemon, and I had a decaf latte.

"My name's John, by the way."

"Bobbie."

"I take it from your accent that you're not from around here?"

She reached over and lifted my book from its bag. She turned it over and looked at the back cover. She had glitter on her fingernails.

"I grew up in Seattle," she said.

I took the lid off my coffee and stirred it with a plastic spatula. The book was a travelogue by a British writer living in Bordeaux. I'd heard it was funny.

"So, what are you doing in Bristol? Apart from working in a bookshop, I mean."

She put the book down. There was rain on the window. "I'm at the University. I'm studying philosophy, but really, I want to work in advertising."

She took a sip of tea. She looked at my shirt and tie. "How about you, what do you do?"

I popped the lid back onto my cup. "I work for the Evening Post," I said.

She put her elbows on the table: "Are you a writer?"

I smiled and shook my head. "I just work in the office. It's nothing special. As a matter of fact, I should be there now, but I'm playing truant."

"Won't you get into trouble?"

"Ah, what's the worst that could happen?"

"They could fire you."

I reached into my jacket pocket. I pulled out the lottery ticket I'd bought earlier. "I have a back-up plan," I said, showing it to her.

Bobbie's face lit up. "Hey, did you ever see that film with Nicolas Cage, the one where he's a cop, and he promises that if he wins the lottery, he'll split his winnings with the diner waitress because he can't afford to tip her?"

I scratched my eyebrow. "Yes, I think so. Was the waitress Michelle Pfeiffer?"

"I don't know, I think it was Bridget Fonda. But anyway—how about we have the same deal? I bought you a coffee, so how about if you win the lottery, we split the prize money?"

"Sure, why not?" I shrugged my jacket off and hooked it over the back of the chair.

"You promise?"

"Yes, I promise."

She sat back. "Okay then."

She took another sip of tea. I tried my coffee. It was too hot to drink, so I took the plastic lid off again and sniffed the steam. Bobbie was watching me. She said: "Do you go clubbing much?"

I shook my head. I was thirty-three. I hadn't been in a nightclub for years.

"Only there's this party tonight at Evolution, and I don't really have anyone to go with, and I thought you might—"

She stopped talking, distracted by something over my shoulder. There was a commotion going on outside. I saw people running up the street in the rain, their feet splashing. The traffic had stopped. People were getting out of their cars. I turned to Bobbie. She was looking past me, and her eyes were wide.

"John?" she said.

I swivelled on my chair. There was something huge coming up the road. It towered over the buildings, a billowing tsunami of dust and greyness a hundred metres high, bearing down on us with horrifying speed.

I reached for Bobbie's arm.

"Come on," I said. I took her hand and pulled her out of her seat. I wanted to run. But before we'd taken two steps, the wave of dust struck, ripping through the coffee shop, shattering the windows and blasting us—and the building around us—to smithereens.

ii.

Some time later, I became aware of a cool breeze dancing over my bare legs, making the hairs prickle. My eyes were sticky. I rubbed them open to find I was lying naked and alone on a grassy hillside, in front of a wooden cabin.

I sat up and looked around in puzzlement. The hill sloped gently down to a marshy river, with further hills beyond. The sky overhead was blue and the sun was warm. There were birds singing.

On the grass beside me were some clothes: a red cotton shirt, some jeans, and a sturdy pair of hiking boots. I slipped the jeans on, which made me feel a bit better. Then I stepped up onto the cabin's porch. The planks were rough beneath my bare feet. There were wind chimes by the open door.

"Hello?" I called. "Hello, can you help me? I don't know where I am."

Inside, the cabin was empty. There was no one in there. It measured maybe ten metres by five metres. It was all one big room, with a bed at one end and a stove and sink at the other. The front windows looked toward the river. Through the back windows, I could see an outhouse and a stone wishing well.

On the bed was a piece of paper. I walked over and picked it up. Printed on it in black ink were five words, which I read aloud:

"Your name is John Doyle."

The cabin's front windows were propped open. The sun cast bright rectangles on the wall. I stood there for a long time, not knowing what else to do. Then gradually, I realised I was hungry—ravenous, in fact, like I hadn't eaten for days.

When I couldn't stand it any longer, I screwed the piece of paper into a ball and walked the length of the cabin to the stove, my bare feet padding on the pine planks. There was a cupboard below the sink, and I opened it, hoping to find some food. Inside were some stacked tins. I pulled one out. It had a ring-pull top, and I cracked it open. I slopped the sausages and beans it contained into one of the metal frying pans on the hob. There were some utensils in a pot by the sink, and I helped myself to a wooden spoon.

The sticky mixture didn't take long to heat through. When it was ready, I took it out onto the porch and used the spoon to eat it straight from the pan. With each bite, I felt stronger and more human. When I'd finished it all, I pushed the pan aside and sat looking at the river. From the position of the sun, I guessed it was late afternoon, maybe somewhere between five and seven o'clock. When the wind blew, the light glittered off the water. I closed my eyes. The air smelled of grass and timber.

"My name is John Doyle," I said. I repeated it two or three times, trying it on for size. And as I did so, I felt my memories starting to return. They were slippery and insubstantial at first, like dolphins in fog, but slowly, one-by-one, they were coming back.

I remembered my address. I remembered the bookshop. I remembered the way the floor creaked as I moved...

I found a screw-topped bottle of red wine in the cupboard under the sink and a tin mug to drink it from. I retrieved the cotton shirt and the boots from the grass and put them on, and then sat on the porch steps again, watching miserably as the shadows lengthened and the sun set over the hill behind the cabin.

As the light started to fade, I became gradually aware of a strange ripple in the air. At first, it looked like a small heat haze. But as I watched, it thickened into something resembling a churning ball of yellow gas about the size of a grapefruit. Little sparks of static flickered over its surface.

"Greetings, John Doyle," it said. It spoke without a trace of accent. Its words were clipped and precise.

I scrambled to my feet.

"Who are you?"

"I am here to help, John."

I backed away. Reaching behind me, I found the rough pine frame of the cabin's open door.

"Help me?"

The ball bobbed forward. It was small enough that I could have held it in the palm of my hand.

"Indeed. You have suffered a grave injury, and I am here to help."

* * *

It followed me back into the cabin. "What's the last thing you remember?" it said.

I put the tin mug down on the aluminium draining board beside the sink.

"I remember being in Starbuck's," I said.

The ball of gas hovered over me. It smelled of ozone. "What about the dust cloud?"

I set my jaw. I guess I must have been blocking it out until that moment. Now, remembering it, my hands started to tremble. I picked up the wine bottle. It was still three quarters full.

"I remember it crashing through the window."

I refilled the mug and took a shaky drink. The yellow ball of gas crackled.

"There was an accident, John. You were involved in it. But in order for you to fully understand your situation, I must explain it to you from the beginning."

I swallowed. There was a sudden hollow feeling in my stomach that had nothing to do with the food I'd just eaten. In an unsteady voice I said: "An accident?"

The gas ball drifted over to the open door. "Do you see those hills in the distance?" it said. "Well, the first thing you have to realise, John, is that there is nothing beyond them. This cabin exists in an artificial bubble ten kilometres across. The world beyond is a lifeless grey sphere."

It was starting to get dark out there. There was a lamp on the mantelpiece. I looked into my mug. In the lamplight, the wine was thick and dark, like blood.

The gas ball continued: "Do you know what a nano-assembler is, John? It's a tiny machine designed to construct things—in this case, computer processors—using individual atoms as building blocks. These assemblers are programmed to reproduce and to keep building until told to stop."

It paused and lowered its tone. "Unfortunately, last year some of them escaped a lab at Bristol University and just kept right on reproducing. They chewed through the Earth's crust in a matter of hours, converting it all into smart matter. There was nothing anyone could do. The human race didn't stand a chance. Within a day, all the cities, plants, and people in the world were gone."

"And that was the dust cloud I saw?"

"Yes, that was the wavefront."

"And what is 'smart matter'?"

The ball drifted back a little way.

"It's simply matter that's been rearranged from its natural state into an optimized, maximally-efficient computer processor using individual atoms as computing elements. We call it 'smart matter.' This cabin and everything you can see and touch outside is made of it."

"So the world's been turned into a giant computer?" I was sweating now.

"Yes."

I wiped my forehead with a damp palm. I drained my cup and put it on the counter by the sink. Suddenly, all I wanted was to get out of the cabin.

I pushed through the door and down the steps. The sky overhead had dimmed to a deep purple, shading to red at the horizon. I lurched around to the rear of the cabin and started running. I ran uphill, slipping and scrambling on the grassy slopes. The gas ball shouted for me to wait, but in my haste, I ignored it. I staggered over the crest of the hill and half-ran, half-fell down the other side. I crossed marshes and streams. I crashed through brambles and clumps of trees. And all the while, in my head, all I could see was that terrifying wall of greyness bearing down on me, ripping apart everything in its path.

* * *

Eventually, scratched and dirty, I came to a high glass wall that extended left and right as far as I could see. I stopped and put my hands on my knees, panting. Beyond the wall, there was nothing—just a flat grey plain that stretched away like an endless frozen sea.

In the glass, I saw the reflection of the gas ball approaching behind me.

"Are you all right, John?" it said.

I shook my head. I was wheezing almost too hard to speak. The sweat ran down my face, and my throat felt raw.

"What," I panted, "what is this?"

The yellow ball dimmed slightly. It drifted over until it was almost touching the transparent wall.

"This is all that's left of the world," it said.

* * *

We remained there for a long time, looking out over that desolate plain, and I thought of all the places I'd ever seen, all the mountains and seas and lakes, all the cities and rivers and deserts—all gone now, all ground down into a sterile, uniform grey.

After what seemed like hours, the gas ball moved toward me.

"Are you going to be okay, John?" it said.

I leaned against the glass. It felt cool on my forehead.

"I don't know."

There was a banging pain in my right temple. My legs felt weak and I was fighting the urge to cry.

"Who *are* you?" I said.

The ball sparkled. "I was born in the aftermath of the disaster that created the world you see out there."

"Do you have a name?"

It seemed to consider the question.

"You may call me Brenda."

"Brenda?"

"Yes. Among many others, I contain within me the memories of a human by the name of Brenda McCarthy."

The ball's yellow surface swirled and sparkled, as if miniature thunder storms were chasing each other across its skin. "There are many others like me," it said. "Collectively, we call ourselves the *Bricolage*. We arose in the minutes and hours following the catastrophe, running on the planet's new smart matter crust, our minds built from scraps of human and machine intelligence, our knowledge of the world cobbled together from the flotsam of the Internet."

It—she—wobbled closer.

"You see, when the Earth's crust was processed into smart matter, every living creature, every building, every computer network was disassembled, and a detailed description—like a blueprint fine enough to show the position of every molecule—was stored in a vast database.

What you see out there, through that wall, is a sea of information, a sea that gave us sustenance as we grew. We took a bit here, a bit there. And for a time, we gloried in the seemingly limitless knowledge we had access to. But later, as we started to understand more of the world before the catastrophe, some of us came to realise the terrible loss that had taken place when the Earth had been scoured of organic life—and we decided to try to correct the situation; which is where you come in."

I looked through the glass wall. The moon was rising, casting its light over the featureless grey plain. "But you're a ball of gas," I said.

"This body has been created simply to allow me to communicate with you. If you find it unpleasant, I can take another form."

I shook my aching head. "It's fine." My knees had started to shake, and I needed to sit down.

She drifted toward me. "Are you all right, John?"

I waved her away and sat on the grass, breathing heavily. "Just give me a minute, will you?"

My head was spinning.

The gas ball—Brenda—came closer. "I know this is a lot to take in, but I am trying to explain it to you as simply as I can."

I put my face in my hands. I felt sick and dizzy. I let myself tip sideways into a foetal position on the rough ground.

Brenda hovered over me in silence for a minute or so. Then she said, "Why don't you sleep? You will feel better in the morning."

I looked up at her through my fingers. "I don't think I can."

"Nonsense."

She lowered herself to within a few centimetres of my temple. "Hold still," she said.

I felt a prickle on my skin, then nothing but drowsiness.

"What are you doing?" I said.

Brenda was caressing my brow with tendrils of yellow gas so thin as to be almost invisible.

"Hush," she said.

iii.

Brenda was there when I awoke the next morning, back in the cabin, feeling refreshed. She was hovering in the kitchen area, and there was a pot of coffee warming on the stove, filling the room with its smell, and a plate of bacon rolls on the table.

"Did you sleep well?"

The windows were still open, and the morning air was fresh and the sky blue.

I sat up and looked out. The distant hills were the colour of heather. I saw a family of ducks moving in the reeds on the banks of the river at the foot of the hill, and butterflies skipping about in the grass.

I frowned.

"What is it?" Brenda said.

I shook my head. "It's the view, it seems so familiar."

She came over to me. In the sunlight, she still looked like a grapefruit made of gas.

"Of course," she said. "Don't you know where you are? Don't you recognise it?"

I looked back through the window at the hills and the river. I squinted and turned my head on one side. There was something about that hill on the horizon...

"Imagine it all covered in houses," she said.

And then it all snapped into place.

"Is this *Bristol*?"

It didn't seem possible, but Brenda said, "Yes. We're standing on the lower slopes of Brandon Hill, looking out over the old docks. That flat area to your left is where The Council House and The Library used to stand—and the marshy area to your right is the dock where the *SS Great Britain* was berthed."

"But the buildings...?"

"All gone, I'm afraid. But if you would like me to, I could probably recreate one or two for you."

I rubbed my eyes. My headache was back. "Let me get a cup of that coffee," I said. I filled a mug and sat at the table.

Brenda drifted down to my eye level.

"There's something else you should know," she said gently.

I wasn't sure I could take much more. I said, "What's that?"

She came closer. "Although we've resurrected you, we can't do likewise for everyone. This biosphere is only designed to support two people."

She settled herself above my plate, right in my face.

"There are those of us—a significant minority—who think it's a waste of resources to use a hundred kilograms of dumb mass—in this case, flesh and bone—to support a single human-level intelligence. They argue that if the raw materials of your body were converted to smart matter, their mass would be capable of supporting many thousands of equivalent electronic entities."

She reached out a wispy tendril to touch my cheek. I smelled ozone.

"Right now, John, you are the only living human in the world. Do you understand me? And you have a very serious choice to make."

iv.

"Do you understand what we need you to do?" Brenda said.

I nodded, although my heart was hammering in my chest, and my palms were damp again.

She must have seen my agitation.

"Go for a walk," she said. "Get some air. Take your time and think it over."

Then she sank into the floor and disappeared with a pop, like a soap bubble.

After she'd gone, I sat there for a while, picking listlessly at a bacon roll, trying to digest what she'd told me. Then I got up and walked out onto the porch, my hiking boots clomping on the wooden planks.

A walk sounded like a good idea. I felt battered and mentally bruised. I couldn't absorb everything I'd been told. I needed to get away for an hour, somewhere quiet, to let it all sink in.

I started walking downhill towards the river, in the opposite direction to my mad flight of the night before. The sun was warm and the grasses and nettles on the lower slopes grew thick and tall. As I tramped through them, I thought about everything Brenda had told me. I thought about my parents, my co-workers, and my friends. I thought about my brother in Australia and my cousin in Italy. I thought about Michelle and the man she'd left me for. And I thought about Bobbie: American Bobbie with the blonde hair and copper-flecked eyes. Was she among the people stored in Brenda's "smart matter"? In my mind, I could picture her face quite clearly. I could see her looking at my lottery ticket in the coffee shop and making me promise to share my winnings with her. And when I closed my eyes, I could almost feel her hand gripping mine in the instant before the dust cloud hit.

* * *

There were no clear banks to the river—the grass just ran into the water. There were clumps of tall reeds here and there. The mud smelled brackish. There were insects circling jerkily in the shade, birds singing discordantly in the trees—all smart matter fakes.

I put my hands in my pockets and walked along the water's marshy edge until I came to the spot where the Central Library had once stood. Now it was a smooth, grassy incline that led up, growing steeper as it rose toward the former site of the University—and beyond that, to Whiteladies Road and the empty space where the little bookshop had been.

I closed my eyes and took a deep breath. There were wild flowers in the grass: things that looked like poppies, buttercups, and daisies.

I kicked a pebble. Nothing here was real.

"I only get to pick one person?" I said aloud. It seemed so unfair. Brenda had told me she had access to my memories and that all I had to do was pick someone from my past, and she'd resurrect them for me. But how was I supposed to decide?

I stomped uphill and back toward the cabin. When I got there, Brenda was waiting on the porch.

"Hello," she said.

I glowered at her and went through, into the kitchen.

"Why me?" I said. "If you had the whole of humanity to choose from, why did you choose me?"

She came floating in behind me. Now, there were faint orange bands in the yellow gas swirling around her circumference, making her look like a miniature version of the planet Jupiter.

"We did not have the whole of humanity," she said quietly. "There were many losses, many corruptions — all of them most regrettable."

I walked over to the mantelpiece. There was a vase there, with fresh "flowers" from the field outside.

"Okay," I said, "but why me?"

In the mirror above the fireplace, I saw her float up to within a few centimetres of my shoulder.

"Once we had recreated this environment, we collected the stored profiles of as many local residents as possible, and you were randomly selected from the resulting list of available candidates."

I turned to her. "You mean you pulled my name out of a hat?"

For a second the clouds on her surface froze.

Then they began to swirl again.

"We narrowed the selection according to certain criteria, but essentially, yes: this was a random choice. The odds of you being chosen were more than one hundred thousand to one."

I walked over to the table and sat. I drummed my fingers on the wooden tabletop. I thought of Nicolas Cage and Bridget Fonda, and just like that, I realised I'd made my decision.

"It's Bobbie," I said.

Brenda came closer. Sparks of static electricity chased each other across her swirling face.

"I beg your pardon?"

"She's the one I choose. She's the one I want you to bring back."

"The girl from the bookshop?"

"Yes."

"That's your final decision? That's the person with whom you wish to spend the rest of your life?"

"Yes."

"Are you quite sure?"

I stopped drumming. "A promise is a promise," I said.

* * *

The next day dawned grey and overcast. There was fog on the far hills and a steady rain streaking the windows. I got up and made myself breakfast, and then went out onto the porch.

There was a figure lying naked in the grass, a pile of wet clothes beside her.

I put my coffee mug on the porch rail and walked over to her. There were drops of rain on her skin. Her eyes were closed, and her blonde hair was bedraggled and sticking to her face. She looked like a creature washed up on a beach.

I stood over her for a moment, then went back inside and fetched the grey blanket from the cabin bed. I draped it over her and took her hand.

"Bobbie?"

I saw her eyes move beneath the lids. Her lips parted and she coughed. I gave her hand a squeeze. "Bobbie, it's me. It's okay. It's going to be okay."

She opened her eyes and sat up. She was shivering.

"John?"

I put my arms around her. I could feel the sodden grass soaking the knees of my jeans; feel her wet hair through my shirt.

"Where are we, John?" She squirmed around, looking wide-eyed at the hillside and the cabin. "How did we get here?"

The rain was turning into a downpour. I pulled her to me and wrapped the blanket around her. Her elbow dug into my thigh.

"It's a long story," I said.

She wormed a hand out of the blanket and palmed the wet hair from her face.

"John, are we dead?"

I hooked one arm under her knees and the other under her shoulders. I struggled to my feet. The rain ran down my cheeks. The grass was slippery with mud, and Bobbie was heavier than she looked.

"Let's get you inside," I said.

She put her chin on my shoulder, looking down toward the river. "But John, what's happened to us?"

I took a cautious step toward the cabin, trying not to overbalance.

"We've won the lottery," I said, through gritted teeth.

The Sun in the Bone House

By Jim Mortimore

"The weary in spirit cannot withstand fate,
"Nor the troubled mind provide help."

The Wanderer
Translated from Anglo Saxon by J. Watson

The bridge at Briggstowe, little more than a platform of rough-hewn wooden poles held together by crudely woven rope, sweats living green beneath a perfect summer sky. Under the bridge, sun-barred, an intermittent gush of brown water slops and eddies.

It is late summer and the air is fogged with pollen.

A child is playing on the bridge. Muddy, naked, no more than eight summers, she throws berries from a pile she has gathered into the river. She has as many berries as fingers. The berries hit the water in slow procession. Droplets of water fly. Something pinksilver and wriggling darts away from the ripples into the shadows of the far bank. The child giggles. Another berry hits the water. The child laughs.

The river throws the berry back.

The child gapes.

The fruit hangs dripping beside the bridge, no more than an arm's length from the child's face. Trickles of water run from the berry, upwards into the air. The child can see her reflection—red hair, green eyes—tunnelled shrinking through every perfect drop. The river boils. The pinksilver wriggling thing erupts from the surface. A salmon, scales iridescent in the sunshine, eyes and mouth gaping. It hangs suffocating in the rose-scented summer air.

Fruit and fish drift higher. The child looks up.

The sky splits open like a wet paper toy, and the future falls through.

* * *

The child, screaming, erupts from the bridge.

A smith finds her foaming beside the river; claims her, wedges her mouth with a stick to save what remains of her tongue; carries her shrieking to the village.

Huts, thatch, goats, dogs.

Filth, blood, terrified stares.

Devil girl, the villagers think.

All night in her, they say.

The smith scowls. *I shape*, he says. *Who shapes does not fear night. Night gives us new wood for our fires, new flint for our arrows and knives. Night gives us calves and ewes and eggs and life. There is no devil in night or anywhere. There is no devil in this girl that cannot be laid by healing.*

The villagers do not listen.

They see only filth and blood, devils shrieking with a girl's voice.

The smith lays the girl on a hayrick under a cool autumn sky.

Bark in her mouth, half bitten through, choking on blood.

More blood from her ears, matting sunset hair.

Bring water, not fear!

The villagers do not move. Furious, the smith fetches water. When he returns the villagers have made a circle. Within it, grass blackens. A chicken vomits blood, shivers, drops dead and begins to rot.

The circle widens. The villagers retreat.

She brings the night, the villagers shout.

Stone her, they scream.

One of them, the girl's mother.

Wait!

The healer has come. He stands, propped on a polished wooden staff, bent but still powerful, black eyes wide, charcoal skin seamed by more than thirty summers lived on shores beyond this one.

The smith is right. The girl has a body, and the body is the bone-house. All houses have a door. What is in her can be set free.

The healer has tools. Knives. Drills. Leeches. Water for washing and lubrication. Strips of hide to hold down the shrieking girl.

The villagers are scared. Angry. They will not help.

The smith takes the girl to the healer's hut.

Binds her with long strips of hide.

Fire. Torches. Steaming metal.

Blades cut. Drills turn.

Water. Blood.

Screams.

A disc of skull, door to the bone-house laid open, washed and set aside to be cleaned and threaded on a strip of hide. The girl, head open to the smoky interior of the hut. The smith, eyes wide, voice gone. Inside the skull, under the bone and blood and membrane. Something else. Something moving. A light. Dazzling.

Sunlight.

Summer in the girl's head.

The healer continues to work. Two more holes, two more doors to the bone-house, cleaned and threaded.

Outside the hut, night comes.

But the sun in the girl does not set.

* * *

His name is Monan, and he is the smith's son. He is named for the full moon, and he has eyes only for the girl.

She is twelve summers now, a third of them mad. She is mad and beautiful. He knows the villagers are scared of her. He hears their whispering voices whenever she is near, casting spells to protect them from the devil inside her. The sun inside her. The villagers punch her and kick her whenever they can. Children throw stones. She never fights. She never runs. There are only words, mumbled through the hide muzzle she is forced to wear. Devils speaking with the voice of a girl.

To Monan the girl's voice is strange. Are the sounds that she makes really words? Monan does not know. But Monan has heard metal talk when burned and wet. Monan has heard living wood speak in the deep forest. Monan knows there are more ways to talk than the words of men.

The villagers are scared of the girl. They have denied her a name, for in a name lies power, and they do not want her to have power. Even her mother screamed abuse and slapped her when the girl tried to crawl home, foaming and shrieking, for comfort, the love she remembered now long denied. But Monan is not scared of the girl. He knows the ways of fire, of metal. The land bows to him, and women too. The girl is beautiful. Her madness makes her glow. He wants her. Burns for her. Moth to a flame.

It is midwinter's day. Ice in the river. Snow on the ground.

Trees, naked, cling, shivering together in the wind.

Animals huddle in pens. The fields lie fallow.

Fires. Smoke. Steam from cooking.

The mad girl is melting ice from the river in a clay pot. Her hair is tangled, one cheek and bare arm bruised. Her face is muzzled, bound with hide. She cannot speak. The ice is for the healer. She lives with him now. The old man from across the sea. He was here before the village, the remains of some ancient civilisation, a stranger to them all. Now the healer and the mad girl are strangers together, and the village swings around them, stone grinding grain.

Monan once thought his father, the smith, might have claimed the girl as part of his own family. But then his father saw the sun in the girl's head. The sun in the bone-house. He made the muzzle at the healer's request, smelting iron, shaping hooks and a buckle. Monan did not see the sun but he has seen the necklace the girl wears, a hide string threaded with three pieces of her own skull, so he knows the healer made holes in the girl's head to let the devils out. He does not know whether to believe his father saw a sun in the girl's head. Does not know what it would mean if he had. But Monan is curious to find out. Very, very curious about the girl.

The day is young and bright. Winter in a child's eyes.

The girl, breaking ice from the river, filling the pot.

Monan watches her from the edge of the forest.

His eyes have seen a different kind of sun.

He watches her until it's clear she has seen him. She makes no sign, but something in the way she moves and holds herself tells Monan she knows he is there. He walks to her. He can smell her even before he reaches her. She smells of mud and sweat and madness and summer.

Her face does not lift from her task, but he knows she is watching him, somehow tracking every move. Animal instinct. He has seen her watch him before. She never reacts. Never fear or invitation. It's one of the things he likes about her. She just exists. As if she lives in a village within a village. A place only she can reach. When she is not shrieking she is very still. Not in her body. In her head. Her thoughts, maybe. Monan is very interested in the mad girl's thoughts. He wonders what they are about. He wonders if they are about him.

He is close now, and still she hasn't moved.

He stops. The river bank is hard, lined with frost.

He holds out a hand to her. In his palm is a gift. A comb made from a cow's shoulder blade. It has taken him all summer to carve it. He is a good carver and could have made it much more quickly. But he wanted to make it right. Just right for her.

She looks up. Her eyes are full of sky. Her muzzle is wet from river-air. Monan wonders if it is uncomfortable. He wonders what her mouth looks like underneath it. He has never seen her mouth. No one except the healer has seen her mouth, and four summers have passed since she was pulled shrieking from the bridge.

The girl steps around the pot. An invitation. Nothing between them but frosty reeds. He moves closer. She smells of summer. Roses and salmon. They meet. He puts the comb in her hair. Her hand lifts. Touches his. They comb her hair together, gently, easing the tangles around the hooks and cords that bind her muzzle in place.

The river speaks then. Ice cracks.

A salmon, last fish of the year, erupts into the air, lands dying on the ice.

Monan cups the girl's face with his hand. One calloused thumb touches her muzzle. It is tight, the hide well cured, soft. Comfortable, then. His hand moves to her shoulder, her breast.

Her eyes, full of sky, locked to his. Waiting to see what he will do next.

He takes her hand, pulls her towards the edge of the forest.

Trees rise naked around them. Wind, a bark-whisper.

Deeper and the forest is evergreen.

Holly, pine, rhododendron.

Naked except for her necklace, they touch, skin to skin. Breath comes hard and hot. Her eyes never close, never blink, never turn away. She waits. Is she unsure? No. She wants him, wants him inside her, her body says so. He touches her hair, presses it to his lips. She smells of summer, goat shit, and roses. But also of iron hooks, leather cords. Her muzzle pumps with each breath. Her skin, dappled with old bruises. The touch of it makes him want to scream. His heart is a hammer, his chest the anvil. She does not move.

His body, a question. She lets him ask.

It's answer enough.

He lays her down and claims her, takes her there on the forest floor, skin and hair and leaf mulch, pine needles threading frantic skin, muscle and bone beating, frantic hammer.

He comes first. She waits.

His world rocks, settles.

Her eyes, full of sky.

She waits.

He reaches for her face. What does her mouth look like? Taste like? He reaches to the nape of her neck. Hooks. A buckle. A child could undo this. Why does she keep it on? Is she frightened of her own voice?

Cords slip. The muzzle curls away, skin from skin.

Her mouth is a rose; her tongue half gone.

Her lips seek his. She's done waiting.

Her body, driving him. He comes again but she won't stop. Her lips are hot against him. Her teeth sharp. The bites get harder. And then he knows. She's gagging herself again. Gagging herself on him.

She moans. He can't hold her. Can't control her. Can't stop her.

She rocks, body stuttering. Eyes squeezed shut. Mouth a tunnel.

She is beneath him, on top of him, all over him; arms and legs gripping, hips and stomach pounding. He can't get out. He can't get away. His chest is burning. His mind, sparks and molten metal, beaten, hammered.

Her orgasm is unending, uncontrollable, incredibly violent.

Sobs become moans, become shuddering cries.

Her body contracts. His muscles crack.

She *speaks*.

"Tomorrow finds you it finds you all dust in the bone-house where—"

—his arms and legs, tangled in her, muscles screaming and—

"—it digs this fine example of an Anglo-Saxon burial site, thought to be you from—"

—her voice, molten, searing his mind, branding him and—

"—the ground all dust and no memories, and the grave of a smith when living, dates from the late 9th Century when—"

—he gasps, breath gone, lungs burning. Later he will find bruises from her fists in his back, circular scars from her skull necklace embedded in his chest. She grips harder. Something snaps in his chest. More fire in his lungs. No breath for a scream but—

"—the body is male and was buried with eyes which do not see behold a palace! A palace of ice and iron and the tools of his trade including tongs and anvil and it speaks, tomorrow speaks to them of you; it speaks and it says iron was a very important commodity to the Anglo-Saxons and those people who were lucky enough to be skilled in working it were held in high regard since—"

—somehow he is screaming, his throat burning with her words, but he can't drown her out, can't shut her up, and now he understands, the muzzle, dear Christ this is why she was—

"This exhibit was kindly donated by a private collector in June 2014!!"

Her voice, an exultant shriek, rips from her beautiful mouth, the fork of her tongue. His mind, near gone, recoiling.

Devil girl, the villagers thought.

All night in her, they said.

But it wasn't the night in her. It was the day, molten summer.

She speaks, and puts the sun in the moon-boy's head.

"You die, Monan, you die and you rot, but they dig you up and put you in a whore-house, in history's fucking whore-house and people pay, they pay to see your death and life, they put you in the City fucking Museum!"

* * *

Seasons pass and the moon-boy becomes a man, with children of his own. Frantic, scampering nonsense. Fire sparks for eyes. Laughter.

The village, slow breath, pulsing. Animals, sunshine, wheat in; children, huts, tools out. Rutted tracks like vines, creeping.

Traders come and with them, disease. Demons from the forest that make sport with the villagers. Children first, then adults. No one is safe. A pit is dug at the edge of the forest, the bodies burned. The sky, smoke black, cold and flat.

Old beyond knowing, the healer dies. He has seen more summers than there are people in the village. The woman washes him and dresses him in his finest clothes. She weaves a crown for him of bright flowers. She puts him on a barrow and drags him to the limits of the village, the edge of the wild woods. She builds a stack of dry wood and lays him on top. She takes a silver coin from an urn in his hut and places it under his tongue.

The villagers follow.

They watch.

She burns the healer with carvings of gods from other lands.

She flings handfuls of summer petals into the fire.

Smoke. Roses. Charred meat.

She takes off her muzzle.

The villagers, retreating.

Her voice, fire-shriek.

"Ancestors of the deceased walk before us, with masks! A coin to pay the ferryman and an expensive procession the *dominus funeri* or designator or head of the Sepulchre for him, no bones and ashes, no procession across the Styx is followed by musicians and women mourning a swift boat across the formulaic inscriptions, no shades to the dead! *Se morti offerre pro salute patriae!* He is a patriotic citizen, a Roman! *Sanguinem suum pro patria effundere!* He is honoured and respected and loved!"

Her tongue is split; her mind broken.

The words, moans and screams.

The villagers retreat.

Charred meat.

Roses.

She sings.

Her voice, molten.

The villagers, moaning fearfully, move back.

Summer storm, the lightning cracks out of her, rips their world.

"*Dea sancta Tellus, rerum naturae parens, quae cuncta generas et regeneras indidem, quod sola praestas gentibus vitalia,* Goddess revered, O Earth, of all nature Mother, engendering all things and re-engendering them from the same womb, *caeli ac maris diva arbitra rerumque omnium, per quam silet natura et somnos concipit, itemque lucem reparas et noctem fugas,* because thou only dost supply each species with living force, thou divine controller of sky and sea and of all things, through thee is nature hushed and lays hold on sleep, *tu Ditis umbras tegis et immensum chaos ventosque et imbres tempestatesque attines et, cum libet,* and thou likewise renewest the day and dost banish night, *dimittis et misces freta fugasque solesc et procellas concitas, itemque, cum vis, hilarem promittis diem.* Thou coverest Pluto's shades and chaos immeasurable: winds, rains, and tempests thou dost detain, and, at thy will, let loose, and so convulse the sea, banishing sunshine, stirring gales to fury, and likewise, when thou wilt, thou speedest forth the joyous day!"

Later, face awash and voice gone to hacking barks, she muzzles herself, watches the healer burn. Smoke. Embers. Molten silver. Honey mead from a great horn to douse the ashes of a man from another world.

Alone now, she weeps.

Smoke, heat from the fire.

Embers like seeds on a forest wind.

Behind her, a sound. Not alone then. She turns.

Monan, face like stone. He cradles a child in his arms. The boy has seen no more than five summers. His skin is wax. Stinking black boils cover his arms and legs. Monan, his voice the whisper of dead leaves, begs for her help. His fear is plain. Fear of the sickness. Greater still, his fear of her words.

He begs her for the life of his child.

Her eyes, flat. Her gaze, expressionless. She listens without moving to his words, perhaps remembering a comb made of bone, given so long ago. She examines the child. He is dying. If he dies, so might the village. She turns from him then, walks away into the forest. He falls to his knees. His moan of despair rising with the embers into a cold, black sky.

Hours pass and she returns. Monan is still on his knees, cradling the child. He has not moved. The child's chest heaves in shallow, rapid spurts. His skin is dripping. His heart nearly done.

She carries something. A basket. In it, bundles of stalks and leaves.

He rises, follows her back to the healer's hut—her hut now.

The village stinks of death.

She takes the stalks, takes mead and rotten bread, scrapes blue mould from the bread, dissolves them in the mead and heats it. The broth stinks almost as badly as the child's weeping sores. She boils the broth until nothing remains but a blue paste. She takes the paste and applies it to the sores. She makes a tea from herbs and some more of the blue paste and tips it down the child's throat. He lacks the strength even to choke.

Monan watches her. He prays for the child.

He prays she will not remove her muzzle.

His prayers are not answered.

Muzzle off, she speaks.

"Penicillin."

One word. A demon word.

What soul will she want in exchange? he wonders. His own? His son's?

The woman muzzles herself. Is she disappointed at his reaction?

Hours pass. A day.

Smoke from the healer's pyre clears from the sky.

The stink of charred flesh, washed away in a sudden storm.

The night passes. The morning sun turns dew and rain to steam.

The child opens his eyes. "I'm hungry," he says.

He touches her muzzle, cups the leather in one smooth palm. Strength gone, his fingers fall to her neck, the leather string threading three perfect circles of bone. His eyes are wide. He knows the stories his father has told of her. The stories of the sun in the bone-house.

She takes his hand, lifts his fingers to her head, places them at the scars where her head was laid open. The child moans, fear or awe, as his fingers find their way into her skull. He convulses as if with palsy and begins to cry. Monan wrenches the child's hand from hers, his face twisted in anger. She watches the anger without reacting, just as she had his pleas.

The child lives; with him, the village.

Later they come, one by one, and in groups.

Pustulent sores and pleas and creeping fear.

Their lives are saved, but their fear remains.

* * *

The child's name is Caelin. He is not tall but he is strong. When Monan cannot work the forge through age it is Caelin who assumes the task. Caelin is strong in mind as well as body. He never forgets what the woman did for him. How his life and the whole village was saved by the sun in the bone-house. He visits the woman as often as he can. At least once a week, and that is a huge effort, for the village is no longer a ramshackle collection of huts but a fast-growing hamlet, and Caelin's smithy is under constant demand for more products. Horseshoes, rakes and hoes, bits for bridles, tools, weapons. Trade has increased between the village and other settlements in the south west. The tracks through the forest are wider, and more widely travelled.

The woman makes her home in three large huts right at the edge of the forest. Caelin oversees the construction, based on the woman's instructions. The huts are foursquare, straight and warm. Their walls made of clay bricks, shaped and fired in a kiln, also built to her instructions. Caelin is amazed at this. The only bricks he has ever seen are those left by the healer's people when they returned across the water. Their regular shape and hardness have until now been an impenetrable mystery. The woman is the only one he knows who has ever been able to make them.

This is the second time Caelin will see the sun in the bone-house.

It will not be the last.

By now everyone who knew the woman as a child is dead. Yet the fear of her remains. She is seen rarely, and then only at times of great need. To the villagers she seems like part of the land. From the sun in her head come looms to make cloth, better ways to preserve food, a special fuel which makes fire burn hotter, so that tools and weapons can be made harder and sharper.

There are rumours that she can make paper, that she knows how to write.

Seasons pass and Briggstowe becomes a centre for trade, popular, rich.

It also becomes a target.

* * *

The first attack comes at night and leaves a dozen people dead. Soldiers on horses from a nearby settlement eager to acquire the settlement's wealth. Huts are burned. Villagers maimed or killed.

The woman poisons the soldiers and the bodies are burned, their horses released in the forest.

Three days later the woman comes to Caelin's hut with paper and drawings.

The drawings are intricate, beautiful, terrifying. Caelin's long hair turns white overnight as his struggle to learn eventually brings absolute understanding. The master smith studies the drawings for three more days, then begins to build.

The second attack is more organised, two hundred men on horseback, armoured in leather and steel, equipped with swords and lances, greed and hate.

They are met with ramparts and staked ditches and towers of strapped wood that fling rocks carried from the river, engines that fire giant arrows tipped with steel, cantilevered rams of wood and rock that crush and maim.

Soldiers and horses alike are crushed, smashed aside by the flying rocks, impaled on stakes, the survivors' throats cut by eager villagers with knives that never seem to blunt.

The soldiers douse the towers with flaming pitch. The wood will not burn.

After three days the army is broken, scattered into the forest.

Their screams linger for days.

* * *

His two sons lost in the battle and his wife taken by drowning many seasons later, Caelin is the last of his family to die. The woman builds a pyre and burns him with rose petals and prayers. The sun in her head is dimmed that day. Caelin was the first person since the healer she might have called a friend. But almost all she has ever known is hate and fear; she does not understand what a friend is.

Life goes on. The towers are dismantled, the wood reused for larger buildings. The ditches and earth ramparts are fortified. Buildings swarm across the landscape, a living tide, ebbing and flowing as the forest retreats, cut to fuel greater industries, and to clear the way for farmland to feed the ever growing numbers of people.

Years pass.

Briggstowe grows from a fortified settlement into a town.

The woman observes the changes as one who tends a garden with care but with only distant interest. Over time her mind settles into a new pattern—a new *series* of patterns. The thoughts in her head are not her own, but then it has been so long since she has been aware of herself as an individual with her own unique identity that the realisation holds little meaning, and no fear at all. Now the image she has of herself is not of a single woman, old beyond her time yet still somehow full of life, but of a crowded marketplace, one rammed with people of all ages, their voices raised as one indivisible hubbub, more thoughts and memories and feelings and ideas and opinions than could ever be held in a single mind.

Though she does not realise it, the healing process has begun at last. Healing and acceptance. Acceptance of the death of the individual she had been, the birth of the new gestalt entity she has become, the sun in the bone-house.

She migrates with the edge of the town, always staying at the place of change, where the settlement meets the forest. From the sun in her head come new methods for cutting and dressing stone, new ways to laminate metal for tools and weapons, for the production of wool and leather; new models of social, political, and architectural design.

From her comes a weekly market.

Trade with Devon, Somerset, Dublin.

From the sun in her head comes the first mint.

Briggstowe—now *Bristol*—continues to grow.

* * *

Time moves on, the days trickling past, sand through an hourglass.

There are more attacks. In 1067 two of King Harold's sons bring an army several thousand strong to attack Bristol. They are despatched with modern variants of the siege engines the woman created more than a century before. Later, King William builds a wooden fort using designs provided by the woman. Ninety years after it is built the fort is replaced with a stone castle, also of her design.

Over the next century, Bristol's main import is wine from the southwest of France, Spain, and Portugal. Exports from Bristol include dyed wool, rope and sailcloth, and lead; the production processes for all these products improved and in some cases devised by the sun in the woman's head. Carpenters, blacksmiths, brewers, bakers, butchers, tailors, and shoemakers find home and work, and raise families. In two centuries the population of Bristol rises to more than four thousand.

In 1239 the woman is consulted on plans to divert the River Frome. The task takes eight years to complete and costs five thousand pounds, a significant portion of the City Treasury. The Frome is a tributary of the Avon; by 1247 the bridge from which an eight year old girl had been playing when the future fell into her head was gone. By then the girl had become a woman and was herself a bridge to times no man, woman, or child alive could then conceive.

* * *

Midsummer Day.

She rises from a dream-haunted sleep. Something has changed. *She* has changed. The days from now on will be different. For the first time in decades she leaves her home without her muzzle. Her voice, feared for so long, will today be heard without fear or prejudice.

She walks slowly along the road leading from the forest into the town. Passing through the south gate, the wall and gatehouse mortared by a process she designed, the woman finds herself sharing the road with a child. A girl, no more than eight summers, playing with a wooden top, a toy whose stabilising gyroscopic properties the woman had incorporated into heavy duty cart design twenty years before.

"That's a nice toy. What's your name?"

The child's eyes are wide, interested.

"Alina."

"That's a pretty name. A contraction of Adelina. A thousand years from now your name will be Aileen."

The child blinks. "What's a thousand?"

The woman smiles. "It doesn't matter. I'm Sunngifu."

"That's a pretty name."

"It means 'Gift of the Sun.' "

"Who gave it to you?"

"No one. Well...the future, perhaps."

The woman smiles. Alina smiles back, not understanding the reason for the smile but responding to it with a child's innocence and affection.

The woman leaves the child, passes through the gate and into the town. The town she has shaped, guided, nurtured, for more than two hundred years.

Childhood is over.

She has work to do.

* * *

In 1373 the boundaries of Bristol are extended at her suggestion to include Redcliffe. Bristol is made a county of its own, separate from Gloucestershire and Somerset. Disease returns, and the woman helps to build the first proper hospital. Leper colonies are established outside town. In 1542 the first Bishop is inaugurated in a Cathedral she designs.

The People's Charter is drawn up.

Bristol is now a city.

Later she introduces a brilliant red dye made from the Scarlet Lychnis flower into the wool trade. The flower, deemed unforgettably red by the people of Bristol, becomes the emblem of the city.

Time flows on, the city with it. Churches, priories, hospitals, pilgrimmages, the Knights Templars, schools. Tin, lead, hides, fish, butter, cheese. The friaries and priory are closed. Protestant heretics are burned.

Civil war, siege, plague.

The grey tide ebbs and flows.

Tobacco from America.

Sugar from the West Indies.

In the 17th Century, a glass industry.

Future Bristol

In the 18th Century, a slave industry.
The grey tide becomes a flood, unstoppable.

* * *

The population of Bristol is now nearly 70,000. The woman lives in a town house, watching with an even gaze as new streets are laid out and built. Queen Square, Prince Street, James Square, Orchard Street; Unity Street, College Green, Cornwallis Crescent, Hotwells Crescent, Windsor Terrace, Portland Square, Berkeley Square. She does not like the city centre. The architecture is beautiful, but there are too many people, and she misses the space she left behind with her forest home. A few well placed suggestions for social reform changes the situation, leading the wealthy out of central Bristol to Clifton. She watches the migration over several years, feeling neither shame nor pride. She has what she wants, that is all.

Shipbuilding thrives. So does chocolate. Imported tobacco is made into snuff in windmills she designs. Cannon, chain, anchors, coal. The Bristol Royal Infirmary. The Methodist Chapel in Horsefair. The Exchange in Corn Street. The first bank opens in 1750, the Theatre Royal in 1766.

In 1768 she proposes a new bridge across the Avon. Tolls are charged for using the bridge. The council promises the tolls will be scrapped in 1793. When they are not there are riots. There are more riots in 1831. The Bishop's Palace and Customs House are burned following the Great Reform Bill. She watches the violence unfold around her. Watches the dead and wounded taken to hospitals she herself brought into being. She feels nothing. Or maybe everything. A white noise of emotion, almost unendurable. She filters everything except joy. The joy of living, of enduring where everything around her is ephemeral, ghosts in time, butterfly lives.

The world, spinning around her like a child's top, turning at her whim.

The city, her City, a toy with which she could never be bored.

Oil lamps become gas lamps, become electric lights.

Horse drawn trams replaced by electric trams.

Railways link Bristol to London and Exeter.

The Royal Edward Dock. The University.

The Guildhall. Avonmouth docks.

A Waterworks. Sewer system.

Clifton Suspension Bridge.

Aircraft engineering.

Cabot Tower.

Shipbuilding.

Chemicals.

Chocolate.

Furniture.

Pottery.

Soap.

Zinc.

Then—

Explosion!

World wars!

In World War II more than a thousand people are killed by German bombing; more than 3,000 buildings are destroyed and 90,000 damaged.

She looks into the abyss, and it looks back.

Madness, so long a distant companion, comes again. A frenzy of mixed emotions drive her to shape and build. The Council House in 1956. The Arnolfini Art Gallery in

1957. The Robinson Building in 1966. A polytechnic 1969 which, in 1992, becomes the West of England University. A Roman Catholic Cathedral. The Georgian House Museum. Harvey's Wine Museum. Watershed Media Centre. The Galleries Shopping Centre. The Bristol Centre. The British Empire and Commonwealth Museum. A new bridge is erected over St Augustine's Reach in 1998. It's not enough. She wants more. More! *MORE!!*

Social reform!

Education reform!

Schools and hospitals!

New initiatives for land use!

Cheap council housing for the poor!

Wildwalk! IMAX! Explore! City Museum!

Stem cell technology! Polycentury lifespans!

Interconnectivity! Free energy from wind and sun!

She wants it all, all of it, her legacy, a new change, a powerful thrust into a positive future, she wants the good to balance the bad, the sane to balance the mad. Her head burns with the helpless desire, the drive, the sheer blazing, screaming, unbearable, unendurable shrieking need for it.

The sun in the bone-house goes nova.

The explosion changes *everything*.

* * *

The 21st Century brings global warming, a Malthusian Control.

By 2078 Bristol's population has fallen from more than 500,000 to less than 5,000. The City burns, a raging infection. Heat, radiation, disease. Rape, murder. Worse. Her solution is ambitious, terrifying. It makes her a pariah again.

She dismantles the moon.

The geological upheaval and destruction from falling lunar debris is appalling. World population is reduced by sixty percent. Animal populations are halved. The tides stop. But the rubble forms a partial shield between the Earth and the Sun. Global temperatures begin to fall. She has bought some time. Time to think. Time for a proper solution. It comes in the form of new ozone, taken from the gas giants, transported to Earth via quantum bridges she designs.

She has saved the human race.

* * *

Centuries pass.

Population growth explodes.

The solution is long-term but very simple.

The solar system has many planets it does not need.

* * *

The Dyson Ring is built in sections just outside the orbit of the Earth and circles the Sun completely. At night, from Earth, it blocks stars from a quarter of the sky. She lives and works there for nearly five hundred years, overseeing construction, troubleshooting, innovating. She has friends, husbands, wives, but never children. She has respect, awe, fear, but never love. Medical science can replace her tongue. She chooses not to. Her tongue is who she is. And half a millennia away from home is a long time. A desire grows in her. She wants to see how Bristol has changed.

One day she comes home.

Bristol did not die. Not completely. And now it is a paradise, the fields of Elysium, Phoenix risen from the ashes of solar fire. Its population is stable at 63, the lowest she has ever seen it, all long-lived eccentrics unwilling or unable to leave the Earth for a greater home on the Dyson Ring. A rural community who grow their own food, understand the balance of nature and technology, willing and able to live in harmony with the land she has shaped. Staggering palaces of crystal, once home to Emperors and Kings, now house exotic fruit, vegetables, growing things, the stuff of life. For the first time she understands how it is possible to love a place when you have ties to it. For the first time she understands how much fulfilment can come from giving yourself wholly to those who trust and love you.

Her ties here are many and long.

Her stories even more, and longer.

She makes the City her new home and never leaves again.

* * *

Millennia pass. Aeons.

Humanity leaves Earth for a new home among the stars. The population of Bristol falls inevitably to one. But she is not alone. She still has the future inside her head, only now it is mostly the past. The sun in the bone-house shows no signs of dimming.

Bristol grows wild and she lets it.

Mammals and reptiles, trees and flowers; genetically-engineered fashion hybrids and extinct species thought lost forever, brought back to life by DNA reconstitution and careful cloning.

Spores, drifting through space for uncounted time, land, germinate, spread.

Hybrids, mutants, invasive species, responsive species.

A new Eden, no carefully tended garden, this, but a wild and dangerous place.

She loves it here, so like the wild woods where she lived so long ago.

* * *

Time passes, until time itself no longer holds meaning.

The lunar rubble accretes and a new moon forms. It is small and dull, but by then even she barely remembers the old moon, and the lovers' hearts whose light the new moon kindles are very far from human.

The sun grows large and red. She sees it and thinks of the Scarlet Lychnis, symbol of Bristol for so long. Wild flower, the sun blooms and dies.

She waits for the starfire, and wonders what dying will feel like.

She waits for the end of things, of life and identity.

The Librarian arrives first.

* * *

The Librarian is a tree.

To be accurate, it is a quantum forest, grown with a specific function. To harvest the past, DNA, genetic memory. To save what has gone before, to savour its riches and grow new fruit, and scatter them across the river of time, that others might taste their past and honour it; so that nothing, in time, would be lost. And everything forgotten would be found and never lost again.

Watching the great seeds fall and burst and grow, she is a child again, lost in a fog of pollen, clapping her hands and throwing seed pods from a moss-covered wooden bridge into a muddy river.

By her great works she has called to the Librarian across space and time, and now it has grown for her and for her world.

When the pollen enters her and she is joined with a thousand, a billion other human memories flooding backwards and forwards in time, she shudders. The thrill that moves her is neither religious nor sexual. Neither terror nor ecstasy. She has no word for what she feels.

But she will find one.

* * *

The moon-garden is in full bloom.

The great trees, heavy with fruit, reach up towards midnight and a handful of dull ochre stars crowding close together, as if for comfort, on the featureless horizon. Movement. Boughs shiver, toys for the silent wind. Stems pop. Pearl-ripe, pregnant with light and memory, the first fruit separates from the branches, falling up into the black night. Ghost worlds, infant geography evolving serenely as they shrink into the sky.

Midnight, unending. The wind blows, fruit falls upwards, the black night turns blue, then radiant blue-silver. Huddled in ancient roots, the child counts worlds as they tumble into the sky. There are as many worlds as hairs on her arm. The child can see her reflection—red hair, green eyes—wrapped around every perfect globe.

Future Bristol

Gnarled and ancient, the moon-tree in which the child crouches fell to earth as a seed from the night. At that time there had still been people, cities, churches, gods; war and rape; love and hope; truth and lies. The moon-tree found root and flourished. Time passed. Now even the idea of time is gone. Now there is only silver. Only the moon-trees in a world of crumbling walls, gargantuan temples to industrial gods without number, nothing now but tumbled blocks swaddled in roots, black flowers cupping midnight, the tiny cluster of ochre stars, tired and still, at the edge of the world.

The tree spans a river, black as pitch, ripples like slow glass. Not water, this. Something more. Something less. A wave in the quantum sap feeding the universe. The moon-tree, a wooden bridge sweating living green. Human memory, seeds tossed by a child into the river of time.

Infant worlds, laced with memory, drift higher. The child looks up.

The sky splits open like a ripe seed pod, and the past falls through.

About the Contributors

Liz Williams is a science fiction and fantasy writer living in Glastonbury, England, where she is co-director of a witchcraft supply business. She is currently published by Bantam Spectra (US) and Tor Macmillan (UK), also Night Shade Press and appears regularly in Realms of Fantasy, Asimov's, and other magazines. She is the secretary of the Milford SF Writers' Workshop, and also teaches creative writing and the history of Science Fiction.

Novels are: *The Ghost Sister* (Bantam Spectra), *Empire Of Bones, The Poison Master, Nine Layers Of Sky, Banner Of Souls* (Bantam Spectra - US, Tor Macmillan - UK), *Darkland, Bloodmind* (Tor Macmillan UK), *Snake Agent, The Demon And The City, and Precious Dragon* (Night Shade Press). Forthcoming novels are: *Winterstrike* (Tor Macmillan) and *The Shadow Pavilion* (Night Shade Press).

Her short story collection *The Banquet Of The Lords Of Night* is also published by Night Shade Press. Her novel *Banner Of Souls* has been nominated for the Philip K Dick Memorial Award, along with 3 previous novels, and the Arthur C Clarke Award.

Nick Walters lives and writes in Bristol, and is the author of several Doctor Who novels, including the Doctor Who Magazine Award-Winning *Reckless Engineering*.

Gareth L Powell lives in the South West of England and works in marketing. His fiction has appeared in both print and online magazines in Europe, America, and the Middle East. His first short story collection, *The Last Reef*, was published by Elastic Press in August 2008 and his first novel, *Silversands*, is due from Pendragon Press in April 2009.

Jim Mortimore slithered greasily into writing as a desperate ploy to evade real work. It was his Last Best Hope for Peace (& Quiet). Naturally it failed. Now he's down with the Narn and the Centauri, hangin' with the Doctor and all *his* buddies, and checkin' out a whole buncha kooky chicks with big attitude or big guns or both and, well, life just ain't what it once will be. Jim Mortimore has been mistaken for human. He has occasionally been misfiled. And while he has written many things, including Doctor Who and Cracker, he most definitely did not write Chicago Hope, as certain weblesque (TM) purveyors of novels will have you spend hard cash on. He knows that isn't true because he simply isn't rich enough. In this Universe, anyway. Life? Here come the BUGS. *HOO RAH!*

Christina Lake lived in Bristol for over 15 years before moving to Cornwall where she combines her day job in Cornwall's fastest growing university library with pursuing her own writing projects and studying literature. Christina's stories have appeared in a number of SF magazines and anthologies, such as *Interzone*, *Nexus*, and

Other Edens, and she is currently working on reinventing the Cornish novel for the 21st century.

John Hawkes-Reed is a Unix administrator. Sometimes this means making the impossible look easy at short notice, at other times it involves stumbling about at 4 a.m. and restarting expired websites. He has split ends and an increasing number of bicycles. While growing up in the depths of rural Gloucestershire J-HR alternated between the John Peel programme, strong coffee, JG Ballard, and "Programming the 6502." In 2006 he attended Viable Paradise, a residential SF workshop in Martha's Vineyard. It was one of those life-altering experiences that usually happen to other people, and made it obvious that he should write a lot more. "The Guerilla Infrastructure HOWTO" is J-HR's first sale. He has vague plans to retire to a smallholding where he will grow rusty farm machinery.

Colin Harvey is the author of the novels *Vengeance* (2001, revised 2005), *Lightning Days* (2006), *The Silk Palace* (2007), and *Blind Faith* (2008). His next novel is *Winter Song*. He has also edited *Killers*, an anthology of cross-genre speculative thrillers and mysteries. His short fiction and reviews have been published in *Albedo One, gothic.net, The Fix,* and *Strange Horizons*—among others; and in 2006 his short story "The Bloodhound" was a runner-up for Ralan's Grabber contest. Colin is a member of the HWA, is the Featured Writer on SF and Fantasy for Suite101.com, and for four years served on the Speculative Literature Foundation's management committee judging their Travel and Older Writer's Grants. He lives just outside Bristol.

Joanne Hall lives in Bristol with her partner. She enjoys writing fantasy, and has been lucky enough to have short stories accepted by a number of magazines, including *Sorcerous Signals*, *The Harrow*, *Written Word*, and *Afterburn SF*. In addition to her short stories, Joanne's *New Kingdom* Trilogy has been published by Epress Online: the final instalment, *The Eagle of the Kingdom*, was published in November 2007. She is now working on a stand-alone novel, *The Leaving of Avenhelm*, which is set in the same universe. In her spare time, Joanne enjoys listening to music and going to concerts and the cinema, when she can be coaxed out from behind her keyboard. Joanne is passionate about encouraging children to read and enjoy writing, and hopes to become more involved in this field in the future. In the meantime, she is always happy to encourage and talk to other writers, and can be reached via her website at www.hierath.co.uk

Stephanie Burgis is a graduate of the Clarion West writing workshop who was first lured to Bristol by her husband, fellow writer Patrick Samphire. Her short fiction has appeared in magazines, podcasts, and anthologies including *Strange Horizons*, *Aeon*, and *Escape Pod*. Her YA Regency fantasy trilogy will be published by Hyperion Books, beginning with the novel *Kat by Moonlight* in 2010. For more information, please visit her website: http://www.stephanieburgis.com

Andy Bigwood is an artist, draughtsman, bookbinder, cartographer, and illustrator from West Wiltshire in the UK where he lives alone, only venturing out for disastrous foreign holidays and the occasional convention. Trained in technical illustration, in Bath (shortly before the evolution of computer-aided art), Andy has provided artwork, cartography, and cover designs for a variety of Fantasy, Horror, and Science Fiction novels including *The Winter Hunt, Subterfuge, Future Bristol,* and maps for the *Wraeththu trilogy;* winning the BSFA Art Award for his cover for the multiple award winning *dis*LOCATIONS (edited by Ian Whates). He has also provided cover art for Immanion Press's esoteric non-fiction titles such as *Raising Hell, Ogam -Weaving Word Wisdom, Charlemagne — man and myth,* and *The Pop Culture Grimoire.* Andy is currently attempting to write a novel when on the train to various places; his website can be found at http://topaz172.deviantart.com.

Printed in the United Kingdom by
Lightning Source UK Ltd., Milton Keynes
142321UK00002B/35/P